Dedication

I dedicate this series to all the readers of the Ruthless Storm Trilogy. It was their inquiry of the girls that made this series possible. I enjoyed writing Scarlett and discovered so much about her while doing it. Thank you!

Books in the Evan's Girls series

Scarlett

Emily

Debbie

Chelsea

Felicia

Chrissy

Eden

Erica

I0725703

The Evan's Girls Series is based on the children left behind after serial killer Evan O'Conner murdered their families. Each story is about one of his living victims – too young to identify him as a murderer. Too young to even remember their families. They are catapulted into lives that aren't forgiving and some find along the way that they have supernatural gifts.

Debbie is the story of her life. How the death of her parents sent her spiraling into a world of hate, racial bias, abuse, and horrifying family secrets.

Elle Klass

Debbie Evan's Girls Volume 3

Copyright © 2020 by Elle Klass
Published by Books By Elle, Inc.
All rights reserved
ISBN:
Cover art created by TL Katt
Editor Dawn Lewis Bookmarks Editing

Author's Disclaimer

This book is entirely fictional. Any characters or events are purely figments of the author's imagination. No one was actually harmed in the making of this story. Many city and business names are fictional as well. No part of this publication may be reproduced, transmitted or redistributed either in its entirety or in part without the author's express written consent.

Part 1
Death's
Seed

Dimwit

The earliest memory is the scent of my mother. She smells like gardenias in bloom. I inhale deeply as if it will help me remember better but there are no gardenias here. I see her smile, teeth straight and white. Her lips red as cherries. The sun on her fair ebony skin makes it glow and her eyes are like dark silk. I know most of that is a fabrication in my head since I was a baby when she died.

A breeze rustles the leaves hanging from the cypress. My mind sees them sway. When I open my eyes they hang still, Spanish moss falling over the edges like a waterfall. I wonder if my mother sat beneath the same trees and imagined life. I often sneak away, whenever I think I won't get caught.

My mother grew up in the house I live in. It's large with four columns in front as if they're holding it up. The porch wraps around it. Inside is a large entryway with fine marble floors that have seen better days. There are many rooms. I should know, as I spend days exploring.

The staircase loops around with iron bars. Glass chandeliers hang from the high ceilings and fancy designs are carved into the molding around the walls, floors, walkways, and ceilings. There's the library filled with rows of books and a ladder that rolls along the shelves to reach the high ones.

Large windows in each room spill light throughout the house. Except the library: because of its burgundy walls and dark wood it always looks like night. At one time the home was marvelous but now it is in need of paint and repairs.

My uncle is a quiet man with no opinions of his own it seems, as he never voices any and my aunt walks around with a chip on her shoulder. Neither like me much. They don't say it in words but they do in actions and expressions. I'm not their child. I'm not even a child they wanted in their home. They took me because there was no one else and they hide me away. I haven't seen beyond our lonely spot in the bayou.

The crunching of dirt alerts me someone is near. Judging by the steps it's Malery, my disgruntled cousin. A kick to my thigh tells me I was right. "Hey, dimwit, where the fuck you been?"

I cringed. I hated that name -- dimwit -- because my mother was black and Malery, like the rest of my family, considered people with color stupid. Although it was better than the other names he's called me over the years. "I have a name, you know."

He shrugged. "Whatever. Get the fuck back home."

He kicked the dirt beside my head. The particles blew in my face. I sat up, spitting the dirt from my lips. Luckily, I closed my eyes in time. He meant business. If I didn't follow him now, I'd get the attic. It was filled with shadows that crept in the dark and loud moans and creaks. It was there I found the locket. It was hung on a long, gold chain with a skeleton key. One side was a beautiful young woman with skin the color of mine. I imagined it was my mom but I really didn't know.

Malery stayed two steps behind me, kicking the dirt every few feet so it would spray on my legs. I didn't say a word but imagined kicking dirt clods into his eyes and pouring mud over his head. I touched the locket under my shirt. To me it was a way of keeping my mom close even though I knew she probably wasn't my mom. It didn't matter, because if she was alive I wouldn't be here in this shipwreck of a mansion living with a wretched family.

I opened the door and was greeted by my aunt. "Where have you been?" she sneered. "I told you not to leave the grounds. If you can't follow the rules, I'll put a chain leash around that ankle." She kicked my shin for emphasis.

I cringed, but knew better than to speak. She was mean enough to act on her words. I ate my dinner at the small table in the kitchen by myself. They always ate in the dining room but I wasn't allowed to join them. I wasn't allowed out of my room when they had company. I dared not try or it would be the attic with the ghosts.

After dinner, I cleaned the dishes and packed away the leftovers. From the window of my room I stared at the moon. It was a full, blood-moon. A gunshot cracked through the sky shaking the house to its foundation.

Shadow Man

Shattered glass and a loud thunk followed the gunshot. I jolted upright and rushed to the stairs, stopping at the banister and ogling the sight below. The foyer window was shot out and glass surrounded my uncle as he lay on the ground, blood spilling around him. I walked slowly down the stairs to see his face. It wasn't my uncle. I didn't know the man. His square jaw hung limp and he was thinner around the middle.

"What are you doing out here?" my aunt snapped.

The man disappeared and my aunt stood at the bottom of the steps. A scowl on her face, hands on her hips.

"I thought I heard something." My voice was tiny as I labored each word. I glanced again at the spot where the man lay. The dull marble floor stared back at me, void of anything but dust.

My aunt's eyes narrowed. "Get back to your room."

She didn't need to say it twice. I turned tail and ran up the steps.

The next morning, Miss. Dresdan came by. She was the only person outside the home I spoke with and that was only because she tutored me while she cared for my grandmother who was very ill. I didn't doubt she was sworn to secrecy to never reveal I lived here. I didn't understand why and often wondered what the world was like outside the bayou.

Part of my studies was reading a book a week. In them I traveled to other places and became someone other than myself. Her voice comforted me, but today was different. There was something wrong. I heard it in her shaky voice. Instead of going downstairs as usual I hunkered against the wall near the iron banister, listening to Miss. Dresdan.

"Something horrible, just horrible happened last night. Mr. Aimes was shot. The bullet went right through the window." She cupped her hands over her rosy cheeks. Her eyes shifted to the stairs as if she knew I was there. Strands of golden hair strayed from the bun on her head.

"That is horrible. How is his wife?" my aunt responded. Her voice lacking any emotion.

"Oh, Mrs. James, she's beside herself. Hasn't spoken since she found him."

A gunshot, glass, and a dead man. *Is that what I saw?*

"What the fuck you doing on the ground?" Malery spat as he walked towards me.

I grabbed my foot and tugged at my shoe pulling my legs in at the same time, anticipating the kick. "It feels like a sticker is in my shoe."

"Whatever." He slugged his backpack over his shoulder and walked by without kicking my leg or shin. Today I was spared. My legs bore bruises in a variety of colors depending on their stage of healing. I stood and watched him stalk past my aunt and Miss. Dresdan to the front door.

"Grab some breakfast," my aunt ordered.

"I don't have time. I'll miss the bus," he grumbled back.

She sneered. "I said grab some breakfast."

He let out a breath, "Fine!" then stomped to the kitchen.

I crept down the stairs and walked past my aunt and Miss. Dresdan. Their conversation had changed. They were discussing my grandmother.

She was very ill or really old. I didn't know which, and at that time took them for the same thing. I was only eight and two-thirds years old.

When I reached the spot where I'd seen the man, the image came to me again. My mind replayed it. My guts cringed at the bloody sight. Last night it looked real. Today the image was faded and see-through. It had really happened.

I finished my math and got settled into a chair to read. My escape from the horrible reality of my life.

A hand gently touched my head and a finger raked through my coily hair. "We need to do something about this hair." Miss. Dresdan dropped onto her knees and grabbed my hands. "And I brought just the thing." She winked.

I adored her. She was the only person in my life that treated me as a *person* except my grandmother. I wasn't allowed in her room, so I didn't really know if she liked me or not. I'd only seen her from the doorway. Her skin was pale as paper. Her hair dark as a raven. They were a contrast to each other. I imagined, when she was young, she must have been very beautiful.

Miss. Dresdan pulled a brush from her bag and a couple bottles. She sat on the edge of the bed. "Come sit in front of me."

I did. She sprayed my hair and ran the brush through my coils that sprang back the second the brush released them. She grabbed another bottle and squished oil stuff into her hand then pulled it though my hair, massaging my head as she went. The motions relaxed me.

"Take a look." She held an oval mirror with worn gold filigree around the edges in front of me. "You are such a beautiful girl."

She'd placed my hair in two ponytails. Each coil separated with care, hanging in spirals that rested above my shoulders. I rarely did anything with my hair and hadn't realized how long it was. A few stray coils rested against my forehead and cheeks, purposely placed there.

I stared with wide eyes. The bands holding the ringlets had red dragonflies on the attachments that reminded me of stained glass.

She leaned in and whispered in my ear, "What's eating at you today?"

"Nothing," I retorted quickly.

She sat behind me with her face next to mine. "How about we go for a walk?"

I nodded.

The muggy air hung around us as we walked towards the trees, towards the bayou. Spanish moss and lush greenery enveloped us and blocked the sun's rays but didn't stop the air from feeling as though it was suffocating each breath I took.

She held my hand. "It's really beautiful here."

I nodded but didn't say a word.

We neared my area, the place I laid under the trees and visited my mother, if only in my head. I wasn't permitted to go further so when she continued walking, I froze.

She turned. "What's wrong?"

"You know."

She smiled. "It's OK, you're with me."

Reluctantly, knowing if I got caught it would be the attic with or without her, I continued, my hand still in hers.

"You heard us this morning, didn't you?"

I nodded, confused where this conversation was going.

"That's why you didn't come down immediately."

I nodded again, my guts knotting up.

She stopped just before the walking bridge. "It's OK." She searched my face and, as if she could read my mind, said, "Did you know?"

"Know what?"

"About Mr. Aimes?"

I shook my head. "How would I know? I don't even know him."

"It's OK. This place holds magic and some people are touched by it."

"What does that mean?"

"That some people have gifts and I think you're one of them."

I furrowed my brows. "Gifts?"

"One day you'll go far away from here. A place where it's OK to be you." The conversation took a 180. "I'm just over the bridge. Now hurry home before anyone knows you've gone too far."

Lonely Cupcake

That was the day I realized I saw things others didn't. The visions came when I least expected them and left without a trace.

Thunder rumbled through the sky and buckets of rain splattered against the window. Lights dotted the bayou, in contrast to the darkness of my life, when all at once they blinked off. Someone closed the lid on the watery hole with us inside it.

I closed the drapes and settled into my bed, drawing the covers over my head. When I opened my eyes next, sunlight streamed through the white sheers. It was my tenth birthday. There were no birthday wishes or cake. No presents, but that day found a way to define my childhood.

I sat at the small table in the kitchen eating my breakfast, a bowl of grits, when Miss. Dresdan entered. "Good morning!" she stated with a delightful smile.

"Good morning," I echoed as she rushed into the next room. Through the walls I heard muffled conversation between Miss. Dresdan and my aunt.

In my room, I worked quietly on my studies, my eyes preoccupied as they stared out the window. The cypress rose from the placid water, leaves swaying in the light breeze. Flowers in bloom splashed color everywhere, meaning spring had arrived. It was the season I liked the most, everything was green and bright.

"Debbie!" my aunt called from the bottom of the steps. Her voice carrying more anger than usual.

I jumped from my seat and rushed to the stairs. My heart palpitating in fear. I stopped cold. She stood at the bottom of the steps, her mouth in a downward curve, eyebrows lifted, and forehead wrinkled. "Get down here now!"

I swallowed hard and slowly took each step.

"Do I need to drag you? Get your ass down the stairs."

The anger in her voice boomed in my head. One minute I was lost in the tranquility outside, now I was thrust into the chaos inside. I picked up my pace until I was standing in front of her. She grabbed my ear with her bony, thin hand and dragged me into the kitchen.

When we reached the sink, she let go and pointed, "Is this what you call cleaning the kitchen?" Pools of water were splashed over the counter and dribbled into a puddle on the floor.

"No ma'am. I'm sorry." It didn't matter that I hadn't done it. When I left the kitchen the breakfast dishes were done and the counter neatly wiped. No, it was Malery. I didn't have to witness him in action to know. He found whatever means necessary to make my life a living hell.

"You'll clean it up, then you will go outside and pull the weeds around the hedges." She huffed as she exited the room with a scowl on her long, oval face. She might have even been pretty when she was younger but all the hate inside her made her about as ugly as an alligator and just as mean.

Pulling weeds wasn't the worst as it gave me time to enjoy the spring day when there was enough breeze to blow away some of the humidity. Bees hummed and buzzed around the azaleas as I sat on the grass and grabbed at the weeds. My mind a million miles away.

"What are you doing?" asked a girl's voice that startled me from my thoughts.

I turned to see a girl about my age. Her smile grabbed my attention because her teeth were so white they gleamed in the sun, surrounded by pink lips and full cheeks.

She sat on the ground next to me. "My name is Noela." She cocked her head. "You don't say much."

Insects crawled along the tract of my intestines as I tried to think of something to say. *Was she real? Where did she come from?* If I spoke to her, what punishment would my aunt bestow on me?

"You don't have to talk. I will." She yanked at a clump of weeds and plunked them down on my stack. "I just moved here. I don't have any friends yet."

We continued pulling weeds for several more minutes before I spoke, "Debbie."

Her face lit up like fireworks over the bayou. "That wasn't so hard, was it?" she joked, leaning into me. "Maybe you can show me around?"

I glanced over my shoulder to be sure my aunt wasn't somewhere, lurking, waiting to find me in the forbidden act of interacting with the outside world. "Maybe." I closed my eyes in apprehension of something, a slap on my face, tug at my ear, threat of the attic, but nothing happened.

"You're a silly girl. I have to get home before my dad comes looking. Can we meet later?"

I opened my mouth to speak but no words came out. I wanted nothing more than to meet her later and run through the trees, take someone to my special, magic spot where my mother joined me but... The shadow of my family hung over me like a dark cloud in a thunderstorm. "I don't think so," finally spilled from my mouth.

"OK, maybe tomorrow?"

She was persistent so I nodded. That gave me tonight to figure out how I would slip away without a major punishment.

"I live through there," she pointed towards the far, woody side of the property. "If you walk straight, you'll find my house. Meet you halfway." She pulled herself off the ground. "See you tomorrow, Debbie."

That was it and she was gone. I watched as she ran through the trees and listened until I no longer heard the brush of leaves or patter of her feet.

Birthday Wishes

The afternoon sun warm against my skin, I bagged up the weeds and headed inside. Water pushed the suds from my hands as they dropped into the sink.

"Debbie," Miss. Dresdan said as she leaned on the counter beside the sink. "I didn't forget what today is." Her eyes twinkled with a matching smile. "Come on."

I followed her up the stairs to my room where a cupcake sat on my desk with a single candle in it.

"Thank you!" I wrapped my arms around her waist in a hug.

"Happy birthday. Ten is a big one, double digits and all," she said, running her hands through my hair. She lit the candle. "Make a wish before you blow it out."

I wished for one day with Noela.

Miss. Dresdan sat on the edge of my bed and pulled something from the pocket of her apron, a little silver box wrapped in a bow that sparkled in the colors of the rainbow. She handed it to me. "Take it."

I took the box. It was so pretty I hated to pull the bow and ruin the magic.

"Open it."

On her words I tugged at the shimmering bow and it collapsed around the box. I slid back the lid to reveal tissue paper. Carefully I scooped the object in the paper and held it in the palm of my hand. It was heavy and solid. I pushed the tissue paper with my pointer finger and it fell away, revealing a coin.

The edges tarnished and black between the thirteen stars. One star was so worn it was difficult to see. A person, a Native American maybe, was in the center of it with a tomahawk. Insignia at the bottom read 1861. I gasped as I looked into her eyes.

Her lips spread across her face in a wide smile. "That coin is magic. If you cup it in your hands," she placed one hand over the other, "you will see things and it will bring you luck."

I lowered my brows. "Don't you have a child of your own to give this to?"

"No, honey, my child is grown and gone. He has no need for such items anymore but he'd want you to have it," she said, her voice soft and knowing.

"Thank you, Miss. Dresdan. I will always keep it close."

She wrapped an arm around my shoulder and pulled me towards her. "I hope so. Now, it's time for me to go. I'll see you tomorrow."

I cupped my hands around the coin and closed my eyes. The image of a young boy with pale skin popped into my head. Immediately, out of shock, I dropped the coin. It hit the ground then rolled to a stop after hitting the baseboard.

When I reached down for it my hand brushed the baseboard and it fell away, revealing a hole. My own curiosity, that of a ten-year-old girl, made me stick my hand into the hole and feel around inside it. Something fell on my hand and I snapped it back as if touched by a monster of the night.

Papers dropped to the floor of the hole. I grabbed them and returned the baseboard. Letters, a stack of them.

Dearest Alma,

I long to see you again. To hold you in my arms. Your skin is soft as a gardenia in bloom. Your eyes as bright as the stars that twinkle over our heads at night. Every moment we spent together, my heart leapt in joy...

Images of white wax running over the edge of a candle, splashing onto metal. Flashes of light bounced against the walls. Two shadowy forms appeared, tangled between the sheets on a bed. The image changed and a couple walked along the bayou's edge under the shady trees, hand in hand. She in a wide-brimmed hat, keeping the sun from her eyes.

Heavy footsteps pounded the halls and the letter sailed to the ground as I was brought back from my trance. In a rush I collected the coin and letters, shoving them under my bed in the nick of time. My door opened wide and Malery stared at me. The image the *touch* brought dissipated.

"Hey, dimwit, what are you doing in here?" There was no privacy for me in the huge, worn-down house.

I shook my head and, as if reading the guilty expression on my face, he cocked his head to the side. "You need to go set the table." He stood in the doorway staring at me, sizing me up, then his eyes shifted to the desk. "A fuckin' cupcake." He entered my room and stomped across it. Snatching the cupcake, he sunk his teeth into it. "Strawberry. Huh next time make it chocolate," he said as he dropped it back onto the desk and stood with his hands folded over his chest. A chunk of pink frosting stuck to his lip and moved when he spoke.

I scrambled off my bed and exited, hoping he wouldn't go snooping in my room. I didn't wonder whose cubby that was or even why it was there. It was something of my mother's. It had to be, there was no other explanation.

After dinner and finishing up the dishes and cleaning the kitchen, I returned to my room, closed the door and stuck my hand under the bed. I sighed relief when the coin and letters were still there. Quickly, I lowered the baseboard and pushed them inside the hole.

The next afternoon I watched for Noela from the library. It was upstairs and faced the wooded side of the house. The trees were dense but I could see enough to spot someone walking through them. I completed my studies, keeping one eye out the window.

The front door slammed and Malery's voice coasted up the stairs. Flashes of pink caught the corner of my eye as it moved through the woods. I hurried out of the study as Malery's footfalls slammed against the steps and hurried to the servant door leading to a stairwell. It didn't get much use anymore but, at one time when the house was grand, it served a purpose.

I hurried down the steps without looking back and into the outside air that clung to my skin, coating it in a moist film. Once in the woods I slowed my pace, following a path that was almost nonexistent. Elephant ears and undergrowth buried some of it. I broke branches and laid them across the most worn areas so I'd find my way back.

Visibility through the thick flora was different than watching from the window. I swatted as the gnats buzzed around me and mosquitoes feasted on my blood. Through small gaps in the foliage I spotted the dark roof of a house and assumed it must be where she lived. Noela sat on the roots of a large cypress. Her face lit up when she spotted me.

"You made it!" she exclaimed, jumping off the root. "Here." She slipped a band off her wrist and handed it to me. "This will keep the bugs away."

I slipped it over my wrist with a thank you.

"My parents don't want me out exploring. They say the bugs will give me diseases and the alligators will eat me if I don't get bit by a poisonous snake first." She said those words in all seriousness.

I chuckled. "The alligators won't eat you if you leave them alone and the snakes probably won't bite unless you disturb them."

She rested her hands to her sides. "I sprayed for the bugs. My parents bought a whole case. The wristband was extra protection."

I felt it working already as the vampire bugs no longer ate away at my skin, sucking my blood. "Where are you from?" I asked.

"Here, there, everywhere. My father is a novelist. He gets into the settings of his books so, here I am, along for the ride."

We moved through the thick brush, following a path. "I wasn't born here but moved here when I was two or three."

The path led to a footbridge that we crossed. I'd never been this far out and was positive if my aunt and uncle learned where I was I'd get the attic, but with Noela I didn't care. Making a friend was worth the risk of getting caught, and in the attic at least I had privacy. The ghosts didn't bother me much and weren't as hurtful as Malery.

Birds sang in our ears and insects chirped around us as we stayed on the path, finally stopping at a fallen tree.

"What do you do for fun?" she asked with a twist of her face.

I shrugged. Fun wasn't in my vocabulary. Over the years I'd learned to hide and stay quiet.

She plucked an azalea and stuck it behind her ear. "What do you think?"

"Pretty."

She grabbed another and placed it behind my ear. "Now we're twins," she giggled. "Put out your hands like this." She placed her hands in front of her, palms facing me.

I did as she asked.

"Now follow my lead. Miss Susie had a steamboat. The steamboat had a bell. Miss Susie went to Heaven," she clapped her hands against mine. I followed until we got to kissing in the 'd-a-r-k, dark, dark, dark' and I slapped the air, expecting her hand.

She giggled. "Let's try again."

We continued, chuckling each time I messed up. Finally, after several attempts, I got it right. "Where did you learn that?"

"School. Sometimes they let me go to regular school. It's fun, but as soon as I make friends, they take me away again." Her eyes dropped, staring at a random plant.

"I don't go to school either. I never have." Hearing her words and the sorrow in her voice should have saddened me but it didn't, instead it felt good. I wasn't the only lonely girl in the world.

"Never?" she asked, raising her head and shifting her gaze from the random plant to my face.

I shook my head. "You're the only friend I've ever had."

"I'm glad we found each other then." Her gaze drifted from my face to the woods behind me. "Turn around. Look."

I turned on my heel but didn't see anything but dense trees and flora, then I spotted it: a roof, it looked like, and different from the one I spotted earlier. We veered off the path and moved through the cattails until we reached the edge of the land. Duckweed and algae surrounded a houseboat. Red paint peeled along the sides and a flat white roof covered the length of it, including a front porch.

We looked at each other then at the houseboat again. The wheels in her mind spun as her gaze darted across the shoreline and water. She bit the side of her lip. "You think we can get across?"

"Maybe." She brought out the adventure in me. There was no footbridge. The only way across was to swim. I held that thought as I spotted a fallen log. "Follow me."

The log didn't quite reach the houseboat and we didn't see any obvious way to get across. That didn't stop us from searching through the swamp grass and cattails for anything that might help our gallivant quest.

As sudden as a late afternoon thunderstorm, I was plunged underwater, a force holding me down. Around me was blackness as I pushed towards where I thought the surface of the water should be, but I couldn't reach it. My hands pawed at the water, my legs pushed from the muddy bottom, but something strong held me down. I couldn't see it, but I felt the pressure against my shoulders. My breath caught. I couldn't hold it anymore. As quick as it started, the vision faded. I spun on my heel as Noela climbed the log.

"I think I can make this work," she said. One foot in front of the other, her hands out for balance, she took a few steps across the log.

"No!" I screamed and ran through the muck. I feared that vision was her death. She'd fall off the log and get caught on something in the water. She paused, weebled a little then guffawed and continued with another step.

"Come back. That tree is old and probably rotten from the water." I reached the end and held my hand out for her. The *touch* seemed to take more than give and certainly meant something like the man I saw get shot. I knew, if she didn't get down, the bayou would take her.

"Don't be silly, I'm a gymnast." She wobbled more, her arms flailing in the air, then she righted herself.

My heartbeat pounding against my chest. The water was too dark from pollen to tell how deep it went, but usually much deeper than one would expect. "Come back, please," I begged.

She tottered more. "OK, I'm turning around." She lowered herself and scooted backwards, her feet dangling over the edge of the log.

My heart didn't return to normal until she made it all the way back. She grabbed my hands and jumped off the log. I stumbled backwards and fell on my butt and that's when I saw it.

Noela

We uncovered a canoe, hidden among the reeds. After careful inspection it appeared to be useable, so we made plans to return where we'd explore the houseboat.

After dinner and clean up, my aunt and uncle asked me to join them in the living room. I'd been caught. They'd waited until now to spring it on me. Even thinking it, I knew that wasn't the case. They didn't pre-meditate punishment but gave it at the time. My aunt would have already locked me in the attic with the shadows and ghosts.

Trepidation crept over my body like centipedes as I folded my hands in front of me and stood by the couch. I dared not sit on the couch next to Malery, and my uncle was in the chair.

My aunt wrung her hands together as if nervous. She certainly had nothing to be nervous about. She then cleared her throat. "Things will be changing around here. Tomorrow I will start a job and from now on will be leaving with Mr. James," I didn't know why she was so formal calling her husband and my uncle Mr. James, "in the morning and returning with him in the evening. Miss. Dresdan will take care of the meals on my direction." My aunt had always been proprietary about cooking. She allowed no one else in the kitchen except me when it was time to set the table. Truth was, she wasn't much of a cook.

She continued: "Neither of you are allowed outside of the house without my permission first." She turned to me, her eyes beaming in warning. "You will remember to never go beyond the large cypress." Her words shot through me as if she knew today I'd wandered off. I hadn't wandered further than the large cypress because I went the opposite direction, so I wasn't exactly disobeying her.

My uncle who was usually quiet and never minced words with my aunt put in his six cents: "You will both be wise to obey or there will be consequences. Severe consequences." The warning strong in his words but I had yet, after seven years, to see them punish Malery.

I gulped, knowing exactly what that meant for me, but his eyes never left Malery, the son who could do no wrong.

Maybe my uncle was wiser than he appeared, something more than my aunt's puppet. Malery rolled his eyes in indignation.

Thunder grumbling in the heavens woke me up. As lightning flashed across the sky, illuminating a figure staring down at me and a large hand clamped over my mouth. My heart skipped a beat as my life flashed before my eyes and I struggled against the hand.

"It's just me, dimwit. Shit!" All the blood in my body suddenly boiled in anger as soon as my heartbeat stopped racing in my chest.

He lifted his hand from my mouth and sat back.

"What are you doing in here?"

He chortled. "Somebody's finally got some pizzazz. Can it!" He slapped my head. "Listen, you heard them. They'll both be gone and Miss. Dresdan doesn't get paid to watch us. Old bat likes you anyways," he scoffed. "Which means I'm in charge and I don't want you tagging along with me. It doesn't matter to me what you do as long as you're home by the time they are."

I swallowed, visually scanning my room for a camera or tape recorder but, in the darkness, I didn't see much but the usual fuzzy outlines of my dresser.

He lifted off my bed and stood over me. "If you say anything or aren't back by the time they are, my punishment will be worse than theirs." He made a sliding motion across his neck with his finger.

The sun rose, spreading the colors of morning over my room. I padded to the stairs and listened as Malery ate breakfast and the front door closed. From the window, I watched as he walked towards the large cypress and continued watching until he was over the footbridge and out of sight.

My ears filled with Miss. Dresdan's hum. Today it seemed unusually cheerful. I peeked around the door into my grandmother's room. Miss. Dresdan brushed her beautiful dark locks, coiling them into one big curl that hung across her chest. "Come in."

With my hands behind my back, I walked into the room. I wasn't allowed inside it but today was different. My aunt and uncle weren't home. I rocked back onto the velvet chair.

Particles floated into the air as she swiped the dresser with a feather duster. "What's eatin' you?"

"Nothing. How's Grandma?"

"She's fine, just fine for her. Come on child, sit with me." She dropped onto the edge of the bed and held a hand for me to join her.

I slipped off the chair and slowly made my way towards her. Unsure of my actions, even being in the room, my guts twisted.

"It's alright girl. No one's here but us." Her voice was comforting and eased my pretzel guts as I padded towards her at a quicker pace and took a seat next to her.

Small webs ebbed from the corners of my grandmother's eyes. "What's wrong with her?"

"Well, I really don't know. She hasn't spoke in years, barely eats. Spends most of the day sleeping. She was so beautiful. Still is." A faraway gaze overcame Miss. Dresdan's eyes. "She could have had any man she wanted but she chose your grandpa. He was a fine man from a good family."

My ears alert to hear the rest of the story. "What happened?"

She took my hand in hers and squeezed. "His family lost all their money. They made a big show of things, but it was all gone and your grandma, she inherited everything. The house, the land. If you cut down all the trees it would extend as far as the eye can see. She was security to him, a comfy life. Well, people didn't divorce then. No, they married for life, richer or poorer, better or worse..."

"What else, what else," I begged.

"This house was something then. Now it's just another run-down plantation. But your grandma was smart, she kept him on a leash and an allowance. Even set things up with the lawyer in the event she ever became incapacitated." The faraway look disappeared. "I'm rattling off. Go on, girl, enjoy your day. Go outside and get some fresh air."

I didn't want to. Her words sparked a fire and I wanted more. "Tell me more, please."

Her lips rose into a gentle smile and she continued. My grandmother had a lover, one she was deeply in love with, always was in love with, but it wasn't right for them to marry. Not a proper southern girl from a prestigious family. He was a working man who barely made a living as a pianist. She adored him and he her. My mother was a product of their love.

I clasped my hands over my mouth. It was hard for me to imagine my grandmother who'd spent most of my life, at least what I remembered, in a bed. A new perspective formed, one that included the secrets of adults. The sins of adults. *Was she Alma?* Maybe that letter was hers. No, the woman's legs in my vision were dark, tan. My grandmother was lily-white. "Her lover was colored, like me."

"Girl, you don't ever repeat that around here. Nothing I told you should you ever repeat in this house." Gloom covered her face. She didn't need to warn me. I was well aware of the darkness settled in the house and their hate for me.

The frail woman lying in bed was something more, so much more, once. I touched her hand and a series of images flashed over my mind but I couldn't capture any of them. Her hand turned and her fingers folded over mine. I glanced at my grandmother whose dark eyes stared deep through me. I saw them vibrant and alive, bright and bold, but now they were tired. "You were always so pretty..."

My eyes widened and my mouth formed an O as I jumped off her bed as if a cottonmouth was fixing to sink his fangs into me.

"It's OK, she sees you but doesn't realize it's you. When she's awake she's not aware. Her mind is somewhere else. Go on. You've spent enough time with two old women. Git," she said, followed by a wave of her wrist.

I scurried down the steps. If my feet had gone any faster, I'd have been flying, and pushed through the front door. I didn't stop until I came to the great cypress tree. Its branches swayed in the breeze and the Spanish moss sparkled like jewels on a silver chain dangling in the sun. I closed my eyes and imagined my mom, holding my locket tight in my hands.

Our Secret

oela and I dragged the canoe from the foliage grown around it the following day. It was sturdy enough as we paddled across the water to the other side. We dragged it up shore, enough it wouldn't float away, then stole onto the houseboat.

It protested each of our steps as we walked across the porch to the door. We took in deep breaths as she twisted the knob and I pushed the door. The hinges complained as it creaked open. Inside, light flooded the small area. It wasn't more than a single room.

Dust piled on my fingertips as I ran them along the table. White candles, long past being any use, took residence in the middle of it. A bed, its purple sheets bleached with age. This was it. The place in my vision where Alma and her lover let their passion take control. It was the place I was conceived. At the time I knew that. It was later in my life I questioned it but, in that houseboat, that day, I felt them and their love for me.

"This is so cool!" Noela exclaimed with wide eyes.

"Yeah." I smiled as I sat on the bed. Clouds of dust puffed around me, filling the air and tickling my nose.

The houseboat became our hideaway, our place. Each day that summer we snuck away. I learned a lot about her. How her father spent his days writing, oblivious to the rest of the world, and her mother spent her days nursing a bottle of wine and popping sleeping pills. I told her a little about my family, but not much.

It wasn't that I didn't think I could share with her but it was my shame, and maybe my grandmother's shame, for bedding a colored man. She was selfish in her ways and foolish. A white woman didn't have black babies. I knew enough to understand that's why they hated me -- my family. I was a reminder of her shame, disgrace, and immoral actions. As much as I hated her I also admired the forbidden love. It was romantic, sneaking off to be with her lover.

I never told Noela any of that but, in the houseboat, I sensed them. The spirits of my mother and father. She was the forbidden child who had no choice but to run off and hide her love. He was white or light skinned, that much I knew from my visions. At night I'd take out the letters and read them, seeing them in my mind's eye. They were in love. A love that took them away from here, away from Grandma's shame.

My mother's full face never manifested in my visions, every other angle of her but never her face, except her eyes and lips. Enough I filled in the blanks. Her skin wasn't dark. A light ebony, her hair raven like my grandmother's and long. She could easily have passed for white.

It would take years before I understood that being colored wasn't a flaw or a defect.

As the summer came to a close for me and Noela it didn't matter. We didn't live by the rules of all other children who attended school. We'd grown brave and decided on sneaking out to the boat at midnight. It was the adventure, doing something forbidden. We didn't quite make it there that night as we heard noises in the woods. Not wild animal noises. Those were everywhere.

The frogs, crickets, and owls made their presence known while lightning bugs blinked from the trees and bushes, lighting our path. Deep moans broke the chorus of night animals and stopped Noela and I in our tracks.

Our gazes shifted to one another and our eyes doubled in size. "Shh!" She placed her pointer finger over her lips then took my hand. Carefully, as not to make a sound and alert whoever it was to our presence, we moved towards the desperate moaning, as if someone was dying.

We ducked when two figures in the darkness came into view. A man, naked, his pants hung around his ankles had someone -- it looked like another man -- pinned to the tree as he thrust his hips forward. I gasped, covering my mouth so as not to be heard.

As my eyes adjusted and the shock wore from my brain, I realized I recognized the hair, the height, and the shoulders of the man. He wasn't a man but my cousin Malery.

"We have to get out of here," I whispered.

She nodded as we crawled along the ground, keeping lower than the bushes. Once we thought we were out of earshot we ran towards the boat. We hadn't moved fast enough or far enough because footfalls pounded like a drum in my ears and twigs snapped but not from behind us.

A figure leaped from behind a tree. Noela running smack into it. She stepped backwards and he moved forwards. "What the hell, dimwit!" he said, his eyes fixed on me but his long, lanky arm reaching for Noela. He grabbed her around the throat. "Spying on me." Rage colored his every word as he moved closer and closer to me, dragging Noela by the neck.

She kicked and her arms flailed then she sunk her teeth into his arm. He hollered and dropped her, scooting over the littered bayou floor, she moved backwards. Anger suddenly covered my fear. A rock, a thick one, lay in my reach. I didn't hesitate in grabbing it and thrusting it high as I stepped in front of her. "Don't come closer, Malery."

He continued and I heard Noela scuttle out of the way on both feet now. "What are you going to do? You think that little rock will hurt me? Huh?"

"Enough to knock you out?" I thought then it was the courage Noela brought me. She wasn't afraid and was always ready for an adventure, but that night she was the damsel in distress, and I was the courageous one. In that moment, that split second of time, all the evil he ever did to me -- kicking me, hitting me, calling me dimwit and other names -- shot through me like a cannon and I chucked the rock so hard it hit him square between the eyes. He staggered backwards and dropped.

Noela shrieked from behind me and the water of the bayou splashed. I picked the rock back up and spun on my heel. She flailed and kicked in the water as a young man Malery's age had his arms around her, pushing her under the water. My vision appeared again. The one I'd seen the day we found the houseboat. Seeing her gasping for air and life made the boiling anger shoot to the top of my head and out my ears. I had to save her. My fingers tightly braced around the rock I jumped onto his back and hit him in the back of the skull over and over.

A rage inside me had been awakened. I didn't stop until he floated face down in the water. Dropping the rock I called, "Noela, Noela," again and again. Frantic, I dove under the water, searching, but she never answered. The bayou had taken her.

An Understanding

From that day forward, Malery and I had an understanding, but that didn't ease the tension. At dinner, from my perch in the kitchen, I heard them asking about the massive egg on his forehead. He claimed he'd tripped on the stairs and hit his head on the corner of the step.

After they finished eating I entered the dining room to clear the dishes. Holding my head high, I smiled at him. He lowered his brows and narrowed his eyes. "You better watch your back. You won't know when I'll be coming for you," he whispered in a malevolent tone.

I didn't back down. I'd killed a man, but he had a worse secret than I since I didn't exist, hidden away in the depth of the bayou. He liked men, liked having sex with them. That would bring shame to the family; to my aunt and uncle. He'd no longer be their golden boy.

A week later, Noela's body was found as it surfaced, caught in the swamp grass. His body a day or two later. The police came knocking on the door. I watched from the filmy attic window as they entered the house.

Stuck in the attic, I didn't hear what the police said or asked, but I listened in and read the paper over my uncle's shoulder. They'd found his skin under her nails and marks on him that matched. Her clothes ripped and him half naked, they determined he was something they called a pedophile. I later learned what that word meant. The bruising and swelling on the back of his head they chalked up to the struggle and closed the case.

However, my aunt and uncle pieced together Malery's bruised head with the time and day of their deaths. I listened by the banister as they questioned him. He claimed to know nothing and stuck to his story about hitting his head on the steps. Really, he didn't know anything because I laid him out cold with that rock. It was the most gratifying thing I'd ever done.

The situation was satisfying as much as it saddened me that I'd lost the one friend in the world I had. I never returned to the houseboat.

Life never returned to normal after that. They thought different of Malery. I heard it in their voices, saw it in their eyes. My aunt and uncle knew he had something to do with their tragic deaths. I was an invisible speck, a ghost.

Two months later, I woke in the middle of the night to a commotion from the first floor. Voices dragged as my mind adjusted to being awake. I tiptoed down to the edge of the banister but everything went quiet. The lights were off. The house was silent.

In the darkness, I slipped down the stairs to an empty house. I stood in the foyer, my ears on alert, my eyes scanning for life. That's when I noticed the front door was unlocked. At night, my uncle always made sure to lock the deadbolt. There wasn't any traffic in these parts of the bayou but he figured if a criminal wanted to hide, the bayou was the best place to stay hidden.

I crept away from the foyer into the shadows of the living room. My heart palpitating against my chest as if breaking free of my body. Someone was in the house. I stood silent against the wall. Had someone done this family in for me, released me from them? Then I thought of my grandmother, the one person in the house I had any concern for, and rushed up the steps to her room.

I pushed the door open. By this time my eyes had adjusted to the dark and saw clearly that her sheets were folded over and she wasn't in them. I swallowed and grabbed the large golden hand mirror with filigree from her dresser to use as a weapon and carefully made my way out of her room and down the stairs.

I didn't know what to do: hide somewhere in the big house, hoping to not be found, or go for the door and run like my legs were on fire. The wooden floors griped as heavy footfalls smashed against them. I turned my head in time to see a man with a large knife. The light of the moon shining against the blood that dripped from the sharp edge. He moved towards me. The mirror dropped from my hand and shattered against the floor.

I didn't hang around to find out who it was, only assumed it was Malery fulfilling his threat. My feet picked up on their own and rushed towards the door. Thrusting it open, I ran across the front yard, past the large cypress and over the footbridge. I stopped only when I came to a cabin and rapped hard on the door.

When it pulled open, I forced my way in then looked at the woman who answered – Miss. Dresdan. It wasn't a shock. She always said she lived right over the footbridge. She pulled a robe around her middle. Her eyes searching my wild ones.

"Debbie, what's wrong Debbie?" she asked with desperate concern.

It took a moment for me to catch my breath. She held my hand and led me to the couch then brought me a glass of water. After several moments I was able to speak. "Someone broke into the house. They came after me with a bloody knife!" I wanted to say it was Malery, but the more I tried to picture the man he was too short and built sturdier. I hadn't seen his face.

She folded me in her arms. "You're safe here."

I snuggled into her. My mind drifting in and out of sleep until the phone rang. I sprung from the couch like a jack-in-the-box. Miss. Dresdan's soothing voice calmed me. "Honey, it's just the phone."

She answered, "Hello, uh huh, she's here -- the door was left unlocked and someone was in the house. She barely got away. Yes. Uh, huh. She's in my prayers, Mrs. James, goodnight." The phone clicked back onto the receiver.

She sat on the edge of the couch, her face grave and her voice graver, "It seems your grandmother has taken more ill. They had to rush her to the hospital."

"Is Malery with them?" I had to know, even though my mind had sorted the details and knew it wasn't him in the house.

"Yes, I believe so. Your uncle called asking me to come to the house since they'd left you alone."

They hadn't 'left' me alone. That was the nice way of saying it. They purposely left me alone. The forbidden child with a black mamma and white daddy. The ghost that roamed the halls of White Oak Plantation, named for their abundance on the property.

I placed my head on her lap and curled my legs onto the couch while she brushed my hair with her hand. A small fireplace sat opposite the couch. I fell back to sleep staring at the emptiness inside it.

Tidbits

I squeezed my eyes against the bright sunlight, resisting its urging me awake.

"Debbie, it's morning, hon. Time to wake up," Miss. Dresdan insisted.

Before my eyes adjusted to the light spilling through the curtains, I smelled sausage in the frying pan and coffee brewing. I inhaled deeply as I sat up. Miss. Dresdan hummed as she stirred something on the stove then leaned over and pulled a pan from the oven -- biscuits.

I jumped off the couch and into the tiny kitchen. "I can help."

"You're my guest. Take a seat at the table, pour you some milk. Gravy be done in a minute," she said, pointing, spatula in hand, at the small table with two chairs.

In a few minutes she set two plates and forks along with steaming gravy and hot biscuits on the table.

Holding the coffee mug in both hands she asked, "You feel better today?"

"Yes." I did but still wasn't sure exactly what happened the previous night nor who it was since it definitely wasn't Malery. It wasn't many people that wandered this far back into the bayou.

She nodded with a smile. "Eat up. As much as you want."

I rarely ate as much as I wanted and nothing this delicious. Oatmeal or grits in the mornings, a sandwich for lunch, and table scraps for dinner. On the little table was a feast. I sliced the biscuit and drizzled it with gravy filled with chunks of sausage. It was an explosion of flavor in my mouth, a delicacy.

"Slow down, child. You're going to make yourself sick eating that fast." She winked. "I called the police and their meeting us at the house. If they ask, you're my niece visiting for a piece."

I thought of my grandmother: was it real? Had she taken a turn for the worse? "Miss. Dresdan," I stared at my plate, "how's my grandma?"

She finished chewing her bite then swallowed before she said, "Not good. She's in the hospital. Your uncle will be working but your aunt is staying at the hospital with her for a day or so. Malery is with her. You'll be staying here with me until things settle down."

I raised my head. That was the best news ever, well, not the part about my grandma but the part about staying with Miss. Dresdan.

The police showed up minutes after we arrived. We stayed out front while they checked the house. I'm sure no one told them I'd seen someone there but made up some excuse or another. It was exciting seeing the men in their uniforms up close, interacting with someone outside the bayou.

One of the cops who looked like he ate too much biscuits and gravy leaned down a bit and met me eye to eye. "How about you, little lady? I think I got something you'd like." He stood and walked around to the back of his patrol car then popped the trunk and handed me a stuffed toy. "These things are all the rage."

The little animal was a pink platypus with a heart-shaped tag on one of its front legs with the lowercase letters *ty*. I thought that was a strange name. "Thank you." I'd never had a doll or stuffed toy but I didn't tell him that. Once they left we went inside and packed me a bag.

Like the man I'd seen shot in a previous vision, I saw the faint shadow of the man with the knife. His face was still blurry but the rest was clear enough. He was mighty short compared to my lanky cousin, real burly, and sturdy like a train. Wide shoulders and very little neck. Seemed as though maybe I'd seen him somewhere but couldn't pinpoint where.

No use fretting over the *touch*. I was more relieved that at least it wasn't really someone in the house. That was the first time I saw the man but over the years he'd appear from time to time, always with that bloody knife.

The next week was unforgettable. We played cards and scrabble. She fixed my hair in the morning and brushed it before bed. We watched TV and I was able to run outside without fear of getting caught. In the evenings we went for walks, counting the birds wading and plucking fish from the water. At night we listened to the frogs chirp and toads moan. Summer was ending and soon fall would be upon us.

A picture of a boy sat on the mantle. I'd been spying it all week and the more I studied it the more familiar the boy's face became, although not as a boy but a man. The smile hadn't changed. I saw it in my mind and heard his laugh. My last night there I asked, "Is that your son?"

Her lips moved into a melancholy smile. "Arvid. Yes, that's my son."

"Where is he Miss. Dresdan?"

"He's somewhere far away from here." She cocked her head, the melancholy dropping from her voice. "Why do you ask?"

I swallowed. Thinking something was one thing but saying it out loud to another person was something else entirely. "Was he my father?"

She pulled my hand into hers. "I don't think so. You remember him?"

"His laugh and his smile."

A tear formed in her eye and she swiped it away as she cleared her throat. "Your mom and my Arvid were the best of friends. He loved her so. His world didn't turn unless she was in it." Her voice shook as she spoke.

"You don't have to tell me if... if it's too hard." I didn't want to see her cry. She was always so kind to me.

"No, no." She swiped her eyes again. "Some memories are sad but good to remember." After a long moment she spoke again. "Your momma, she met a man who took her away from this place, out into the world. He rescued her. My Arvid understood she didn't feel about him the way he felt about her. She married that man and had children, but he passed -- drunk driver the way I heard it. Anyways, my Arvid reached out to her and picked up the pieces. In almost every way, he was a daddy to you and your--" She stopped cold.

"My who?" She couldn't leave me hanging there. I just had to know.

She squeezed my hands tight. "You can't ever breathe a word of this."

I nodded and she knew I was good for it.

"Your brothers."

I had brothers? "Where, where are they?"

Her voice cracked. "They're all dead honey. You were the only one spared. I don't know why but that's when you were brought to White Oak Plantation."

My mind was spinning in circles. My heart thrashing in pain. "Why them? Why not you? You're my grandmother too."

"No, sweetie, I don't think I am. By the time your mother finished mourning your father and started listening to her body she understood right away that she was pregnant with you. My Arvid had only arrived and reached out to her but in every other way he was your daddy." She let my hands go and placed her hands on my cheeks. "He loved you."

The coin she gave me was his. Cupping it in my hands took me to him, memories of him. Not my memories, but those trapped in the coin. I leaned in closer. "But why not you?"

Her brows squeezed in tight and wrinkles swept across her forehead. "Why not me?"

"Why didn't I come live with you?"

"I'm not your grandmother, but I tried. Once your family heard what happened. They snatched you up. The only thing I could do to be close to you was work for them." She caressed my cheeks.

"What about my real daddy? Didn't he have family?" I asked in desperation.

"His parents were dead but he had siblings. They were too young to take on a child. They weren't much more than children themselves." Her eyes searched mine.

My breath caught in my throat and tears rolled down my cheeks. I still didn't understand why my aunt and uncle wanted me. They had no love for me. I had something else now -- a family somewhere. I leaned against her chest and cried. She held me against her and leaned her head on mine.

I nearly broke down in tears again the next day when Miss. Dresdan told me I had to return home. The salty water rose to the corners of my eyes and threatened to fall over my cheeks.

Life Can Improve

ife became easier when Grandma returned home. She had a spell, a bad one, but was on the mend. Each day she was stronger and better than the previous day. Her health was on the upturn, better than it had been in years. She insisted I eat at the table and take her for walks. My aunt and uncle treated me good when she was around and I was able to leave the house.

Most of the time, Grandma called me Alma. Her memory wasn't so good but her health was in a constant state of improvement. I didn't know what they did to her in that hospital but it worked.

"We're going into town today," Grandma said with a squeeze of my hand and a wink.

My aunt froze and a flare of resentment flashed over her eyes before her mouth twisted into a fake smile. "A great idea. I could use a few things from the store."

Grandma's dark eyes stared hard at my aunt. "Not you. I'm taking the child. She needs to see something outside this place and her room looks like slave quarters." Irritation mixed with something else, something menacing, filled her words.

I sniggered inside, careful not to let it out as my aunt would surely find a way to pay me back when Grandma wasn't watching.

"Why don't you clean this place? It was always so grand, sparkling lights, shining floors. In my youth a white glove wouldn't have found a speck of dust. Your housekeeping skills leave much to be desired. Start with the moldings, dust and dirt caked inside them. We aren't pigs." Grandma patted a napkin around the edges of her mouth then set it down. She turned to me. "Go, put on your best."

I didn't have a best, most of my shorts were cut-offs from jeans I'd grown out of and my shirts were plain. I had not one dress. I whispered in her ear. I felt my aunt listening, eavesdropping on my words. "I don't have anything nice."

"Fiddlesticks, we'll take care of that. Go on, get dressed," she ordered.

A car came for us. It was big with soft seats. Small gadgets gleamed from the dash and door panels. I'd never in my life been inside a car that I could remember and most definitely not one this fine and luxurious. The driver even held the doors open for Grandma, Miss. Dresdan, and myself before he folded Grandma's wheelchair and placed it in the trunk.

I wasn't sure why she'd brought the wheelchair, she rarely used it anymore, but guessed her strength hadn't fully returned.

The dirt road followed twists and bends lined with large, leaning cypress and white oaks, low bridges met the edge of the mirrored water. It felt like an hour had passed before the road met pavement. For the first time I soaked in the quintessential beauty surrounding us.

My grandmother pointed out the large plantations that popped up between the smaller cabins like the one Miss. Dresdan lived in. She was filled with family names and memories. All meant nothing to me. It must have been another hour or so before we reached an area filled with smaller homes, crammed together like sticks in a bag. The road smoothed out and filled with cars and people, leaving the swamp and its bad memories behind us.

Two-story brick buildings and store fronts ran along the edge of every sidewalk, metal awnings dropped from their second floors. Some had balconies that spanned the second and even third floors with square or rounded frames. Lights hung across the streets at every intersection. People milled about, chatting, walking, entering and exiting stores and restaurants.

Once the driver stopped he came around and opened our doors, helping my grandmother into her wheelchair. Miss. Dresdan took over from there. They talked as I gawked at the world around me. I didn't have any recollection of it.

Not thinking were I was headed, only following Grandma and Miss. Dresdan, we entered a store filled with beautiful, colorful fabric curtains and bed ensembles. Trinkets sat on furniture in tiny rooms with beds.

Grandma spoke but I didn't quite hear her as my eyes and mind were filled with wonder. Her dark eyes glanced up at me and the second time I caught her words, "I said, anything you want, dear?"

Me? I could choose? There was so much beauty I didn't know where to start. As if she read my mind she pointed towards a fluffy white comforter with silver crisscrosses and buttons where they met. Several matching pillows rested against the headboard.

I was speechless as I moved towards the fabulous ensemble. I ran my finger along the edge when something else caught my eye. A bed ensemble, red as a cherry. Its ruffles woven into a circle that grew larger from the middle to the edges.

Her eyes on mine, Grandma said, "You like that one?"

I nodded, "Yes, oh yes," and ran towards it. The cotton fabric softer than a bunny's fur.

From there she ordered me a new bed with a headboard and matching dresser with a large mirror. The paint was discolored at the edges as if an antique, yet it was brand new. After, we went to lunch in a restaurant filled with treasures that hung on the wall in the form of pictures and murals. Large white columns ran the length and an angel spilled water from her mouth into a large basin in the center. Dark colors offset by light trim graced each wall.

"Aren't you hungry?" Miss. Dresdan asked after our food arrived.

She shook my mind from its wonder. "Yes, yes."

My grandma shook her head and mumbled something that sounded precariously like, "Darn daughter of mine."

I quit stirring my food mindlessly with my fork, in complete awe of my surroundings, and took a bite. It melted on my tongue and the flavors danced a jig in my mouth. My aunt's cooking was nothing this grand, in fact everything she made was bland, boring. This had bite and personality.

Stuffed with a fine lunch, Grandma took me to one more store where I picked out a whole new wardrobe filled with designer jeans and blouses, even summer dresses, and silk underwear. She bought me real shoes, not jelly sandals and flip flops, but real shoes.

The long car ride back to the bayou lulled me to sleep. I woke up in my bed, whispered voices echoed through the halls and snuck under my door, filling my ears.

"It's happening all over again, repeating and repeating. I can't do this anymore," my aunt's voice pleaded as I'd never heard before. It was soft and sorrowful, not hard and tight.

"We don't have a choice. Where else are we going to go? You are her daughter. The only one that counts. The only one that's alive. You can do this," my uncle said, his voice fierce. It was as if they switched roles.

"That's all you want, and that girl. I see the way you look at her. Don't you dare because I will force you from this home with your life." Her words filled with threat. Their roles now switched again, switched to normal.

Pins and Pokes

ate summer after my twelfth birthday, I sat on the edge of the footbridge. My feet dangling over the water and my hands rested against the wooden bars. The clouds moved over the glassy water, reflecting back into the sky. Malery's familiar footfalls moved towards me. My days of fearing him ended when Grandma's health returned, but even she couldn't erase the demons of our past.

He scooted beside me, laying something down close to his leg opposite me. "I haven't always liked you. I still don't like you. I live with you because I have to. I have a chance now to leave this place, and I won't look back, but you have to do something for me." He'd grown so tall and his lankiness morphed into definition.

I couldn't imagine what I could do for him and had no mind to do anything for him. Him going off to college was a good thing. It took him out of my life and I hoped it was permanent. "What can I possibly do for you?"

He lowered his head and stared at the water. "Keep our secret. Grandma loves you, not me. She only agreed to pay for my college if my mom agreed to give up her share of Grandma's money."

I cocked my head. "What do you mean?"

"I mean," his voice shook, "if grandma finds out who I am, what I am, my college tuition is gone and my parents are out, homeless." The quiver in his voice made me want to believe him but if any of that was true why did they still live here?

Why didn't they leave long ago? Grandpa must have left her something. She was his child. Then I remembered Miss. Dresdan's words about Grandma. The fortune, the money, was hers but he must have had something. Surely a wealthy single woman wouldn't have married a pauper. "And what if I tell?"

"Don't get cocky. Maybe I can't tell anyone what you did even though I know you killed him." He pulled a little cloth doll from beside his leg. "I warned you then to keep our secret. This doll is spelled with voodoo. If I find that you said anything to anyone I will break its neck." He wrapped his fingers around the doll's stuffed neck and squeezed.

As if by power of suggestion, my lungs tightened and I gasped for air. An inferno, hot as hellfire, burned around me. My feet and arms tied to bedposts. No, not my feet and arms but someone else's. Their face blurred. Each breath I inhaled filled my throat and lungs with ash and I gasped again and again. The vision faded and Malery stared at me wild-eyed.

"That shit really works!"

I lowered my brows. It wasn't the doll at all but the *touch* showing me his fiery death of oxygen deprivation. "I'm not telling anyone. If I was going to I'd have already done it." It was better to let him think he had the upper hand and how could anyone give another person details about their death. Even I wasn't so cruel to the person I hated most.

Once he and the silly doll left, I lifted myself up and walked to the large cypress. A new chapter in my life was emerging, better than the previous one. I likened it to a fairy tale, even fairy tales have darkness.

When winter came, Grandma had us all cleaning and primping the house. We covered it in lights that sparkled over the water and ornaments of all sizes inside and out. Grandma decided it was time to celebrate and was feeling at ninety percent, she insisted.

The night of the party I put on one of the pretty bras she bought me and matching silk underwear. Over that I pulled on a red velvet dress and slipped my feet into shiny black shoes with a small heal. Grandma bought me the finest and prettiest. I felt like a girl and glancing at my reflection in the mirror I barely recognized the young woman I'd grown into.

Miss. Dresdan pulled my hair up into a ponytail with a red bow that matched my dress and Grandma insisted I wear her lipstick. She swiped it across my bottom lip. "Press down and do this," she said as she moved her lips together. When I was done, my lips reminded me of my mother's, full and red like a cherry. The color brought out the dark of my eyes.

People I certainly didn't know milled about the great house, staying mostly in the large living room and ballroom. Grandma hired what she called caterers. Dressed in tuxes and black skirts with white tops, all of them with Santa hats, served drinks and snacks they called hors d'oeuvres. Such a strange name for food.

Wine and champagne flowed and I snuck one or two glasses. Every time I saw my uncle he had at least one glass, sometimes two, but so did everyone else except my aunt, and Grandma sipped slow, nursing each drink. I was the only person in the house under the age of about thirty, even Malery hadn't come home from school yet. Really it was quite boring but also exciting as I wasn't the ghost child roaming the miserable home alone, always on the lookout for her evil cousin.

"And who are you?" asked a gentleman wearing a sweater with lights that blinked on and off. I was so fascinated by them I didn't get a look at his face.

I thought about his question. It was a catch twenty-two. If I answered honestly, would I get punished? If I lied, what was the lie I was to tell? No one had told me who I was that night. I stared at the lights on his shirt blinking as if telling a secret message.

"This is Debbie. My grandchild," my grandma said and wrapped an arm around my shoulder.

I choked on my spit. She had gotten my name right and admitted to an outsider that I was related to her. And in her voice I sensed pride. Lifting my gaze from the blinking lights, I stared at her. She gazed at the man, a smile on her face. Small lines ebbed from her lips to her eyes.

I then glanced at the man. His blue eyes soft as sky and every bit as warm and inviting. "Nice to meet you, Debbie. I have a boy about your age." His eyes shifted from me to my grandmother. "If I'd have known I'd have brought him. The bayou can be a lonely place."

Grandma unwrapped her arm from my shoulder and grabbed both of his. "Next time you be sure to do that." After that, they talked adult stuff. I was still in shock and wished he'd have brought his son. It would sure have been nice to have someone else young like me to hang out with.

The party drew long and I slipped into my room and brought out my mom's letters. As I read for the first time I felt it didn't feel right, like I was peeping at a couple through a window. I put them away, changed into a nightgown, and dropped onto my fluffy bed.

A shift in my bed carried me out of my sleep. Still drowsy, I snuggled on my side and closed my eyes again until a hand slipped over my right breast. My arm swung back and my elbow hit flesh and a loud wail resounded through my ear. It was a reflex and a good one. Someone was in my bed beside me. My breath caught and panic bolted through me like lightning. All I could do was leap out of it and, thrusting my door open, I flew towards the stairs.

Unsteady footfalls against the wooden floors echoed behind me as I reached the steps. Without looking, I rushed down them and towards the front door. My plan wasn't to stop until I reached Miss. Dresdan's and I was nearly at the door when an earth-shattering thud hit the floor.

My hand reaching for the doorknob, I glanced behind me and on the floor was my uncle, a bloody puddle surrounding his head. My eyes progressed upwards, ending when they spotted my aunt standing by the iron railing. When she caught my eye, she gasped and placed a hand over her mouth. It happened so quick I didn't think more about it then.

This scene was familiar to me. My very first vision I saw my uncle fall over the railing and hit the ground. Another man died that night and the vision changed and I saw him die too. I saw them both like a double vision.

She rushed down the stairs then glared at me. "Don't stand there gawking. Get the phone!" she screamed.

I swallowed and did as she asked. My grandma soon joined us. For the first time, I felt not like an outsider but an intruder. The narrowed eyes, raised brows, and eye-sword jousting between my grandma and aunt said so much without any words being said.

"Debbie, dear," Grandma said, taking my hands in hers. "I think it would be wise for you to go up into the attic, just for a bit." She winked.

I gulped. *Her too?* "I can go to Miss. Dresdan's. I know the way," I suggested in desperation. I didn't want to go into the attic. I thought those days were over and we lived so far away from everyone I'd have plenty of time to get there before the police arrived.

"It would be best--"

I cut her off, "Really, I can run fast. I'll be there long before anyone gets to the house."

Grandma let out a deep breath. "Honey, it's best for you to go to the attic." Her velvety eyes stared into mine. "They'll want to talk with Miss. Dresdan since she was here tonight and... You're safer. Now go." She waved me on.

I glanced to my aunt. There was a satisfaction in her eyes that dug into me like deep blades. Dragging myself, shoulders drooped, up the stairs I stopped when I came to the attic door with its deep artsy grooves. I stared over my shoulder and spotted my aunt coming up the final flight of steps.

The door was heavy as I pushed it open. Dust particles filled my nostrils, and the lingering odor of mothballs and mildew. A familiar scent I hadn't smelled in years came back like a long-lost friend. The door automatically closed behind me. I used the existing light from the hall that lessened each second as the heavy door fell into place. The moonlight and starlight gleamed through the window. Between the two I found my way to the stoop where I sat, pulled up my knees, and stared into the night.

Metal bolts rolled into place as my aunt locked the door. The shadows stayed out of the light. Strange forms that appeared as monsters were nothing more than covered furniture. With my shirt over my nose I sucked in a deep breath and watched out the window, ignoring the creeping ghosts and whispering secrets.

The window was tall and narrow. Caked and peeling paint surrounded the glass. It was my grandma, not my aunt, that locked me up this time. A betrayal that stung and festered as I stared blankly into the moonlight. Fog rose over the water, blanketing the land. It did little to comfort me.

Grandma... not the person I thought she was. I'd considered her an ally, an adult that considered me human. At the party I wasn't hidden but shown off and called *my granddaughter*. A false security, it was. An envelope of lies. Tears rolled over my cheeks and snot clogged my nose.

Lights finally flashed through the soft, misty air - their edges fuzzy. I watched on as the commotion below happened. Mouths opened and words I couldn't hear came out. From this distance and through the moist air it was impossible for me to read their lips. I thought she was on my side, yet *she* put me in the attic too.

It was the time I spent up there sitting in the window alcove that the surreal events of the night circulated my brain. My uncle was drunk, he slipped into my bed. *Did he know it was mine or did he think it was his?* Something private was

going on between my aunt and grandma -
- something long-standing.

Light broke through the fog as
the sun made its appearance, chasing
away the shadows. My fear lessened and
my curiosity increased as I slipped off the
stoop. Whatever was between them
might be hidden away in the centuries-
old piles of stuff in the attic. I could be
looking at their secret.

I sifted, sorted, and climbed
through the blanketed furniture. Brushing
the century or so of dust off an old,
cypress, hand-carved chest, I lifted the
lid. A yellowed dress with frills, ruffles,
and lace filled it. Pulling the dress out
carefully. It was flouncy with a low-cut
bodice. No doubt a wedding dress. My
grandmother's maybe, maybe older than
her.

I folded it as best I could and
placed it back into the box then went on
to another and then another. All sorts of
treasures filled the attic. Pictures of my
ancestors yellowed from age in their
high-collared shirts and dresses. Adorned
in vests and cufflinks. They looked like
walking dollar bills. Never in all my visits
into the attic did I rummage through its
secrets, not like I was today.

For the moment I forgot about
the night's events until coming across a

picture of my grandma in her youth, arm wrapped inside a man's arm. I guessed he was my grandfather, although not my real blood one but the one who married Grandma. Beside him was my uncle, and my aunt in front of him. Another woman with light ebony skin stood in front of my grandfather. My mother -- her cherry red lips pouty and her eyes forlorn. The entire group was absent of smiles as if forced to pose.

I clutched the locket around my neck. My mother. I felt incredibly close to her in that moment. My eyes never leaving the photo, they drifted over my uncle. His face was smooth and young. Staring into his eyes, flashes of my memories of him bounced through my head. The entire scene played again and again as I attempted to piece together my uncle's death.

The sun's light moved across the attic as if mocking how long I'd been stuck here. Its glow rested on a gold object behind the large cypress chest. I moved closer to get a better look – a doorknob. Below the alcove was a small door. Pressing my small body into the chest and bracing my feet on the dusty wood floor I shoved the chest out of the way. Intense fear and curiosity rose inside me as I tried the knob. It was locked.

Then I remembered the key that rested on my chest beside the locket. It was an old skeleton key, probably opened all the doors in the house decades ago, but now it opened nothing except maybe the door lock in front of me.

On my knees, the knob was chest high. Carefully pulling the chain from around my neck I pushed the key into the lock on the door. It fit and turned. I inhaled a deep breath and blew it out slowly. Whatever mysteries lay beyond the door, in whatever room was there, its contents hadn't been seen in many, many years.

The door creaked and moaned on its hinges as I pushed it open. Light flooded the dark room, spilling over the dusty wooden floor. The room was completely void except for a single large, cypress trunk. I crawled through the doorway, towards the trunk.

I lifted the lid expecting more family memories, instead it was empty. I shoved it out of the way with ease. As my sixth sense had suspected there was a crawl space behind it. The light shining from the attic window illuminated steps. Only a petite person could fit through the space.

All sorts of crazy thoughts went through my head. *Did my ancestors use this room for punishment? Hiding their black children away for no one to find and shame them?* I knew it would have been my room if my aunt knew of its existence. *Was it a secret escape for someone? Where did it go, another room, outside, another secret passage?* I'd come this far and decided I might as well continue my exploration.

Carefully, I turned around and backwards crawled through the space. My feet finding the steps, I continued pushing backwards until my hands reached the railing then persisted in my descent into the unknown bowels and secrets of the house.

When my feet reached the bottom and solid ground, I released my grip on the railing, my heart racing at the speed of light, and attempted to focus in the darkness. I groped the walls for a light switch but found none. Short of panic I found a slim crease in the wall. I felt along it with my hands. Convinced it was a door, I pushed against it. Disheartened, I leaned my back against the wall. Old wood and dust filled my nostrils as I'd stirred whatever inhabited this room.

My eyes adjusting to the darkness made out forms in the middle of the room. Cautiously I padded closer, my eyes struggling to understand what they were seeing. I pressed my hand against a cold, metal object. Men, darker than me, filled the room, mixing, pouring, lifting wooden barrels. Whispers filled the space, surrounding me in secrets I couldn't understand as if spoken in a different language. In shock, I stepped backwards, falling against the floor, releasing my touch on the object, halting my vision before I saw whatever death was attached to it. My breaths shallow as the men disappeared and the door opened.

I pushed onto my feet and rushed towards the door, welcoming the stream of light as it bathed my skin. I was in the servant hall. The hidden door was flush with the seam between walls and completely invisible, explaining how it stayed hidden all these years. I opened the door, my lungs welcoming the fresh cool air over the stuffy, musty air of the hidden room and attic.

I crept along the side of the house and pressed my frame against the side and listened. Their voices carrying well in the still air. My aunt explained what happened. How she heard a scream, probably when I hit him with my elbow. He, undoubtedly to me, was the stranger in my bed. After she got up and noted he wasn't in bed put on her robe and exited her room in time to see him fall over the banister without enough time to stop it from happening.

It was a believable story. I peeked my face around the corner and lowered to my hands and knees, using the bushes around the front of the house for cover. My aunt never shed a tear. Her lips scrunched and forehead wrinkled, she appeared angry. Maybe shock, but even so she was very alert and wasted no time in locking me in the attic. What was so normal for so many years now seemed dysfunctional. *Who locks a child in the attic?*

My uncle's body was loaded into the back of a car and the police filed into their car following my uncle's body out of the bayou. Grandma held my aunt from behind. Her hands rested on her shoulders. Never did those two show affection for one another. My aunt turned on her heel, my grandmother looped her arm around my aunt's -- her face red and puffy.

Did she cry and put on a show for the police? Maybe it was a delayed reaction. No, my grandmother clearly did not approve of my uncle.

Remembering they'd left me in the attic I scurried inside the house and into the hidden room. I had to return so they didn't find out the little secret I discovered about the house. Worse, no doubt I'd be in trouble and maybe they'd lock me in the room to shrivel and die.

I pushed the hidden door closed, darkness blanketing me, and felt along the wall for the ladder that would lead me back upstairs. I hurried, attempting to maintain my footing on the small steps. Light shone against my head as I ascended and scrambled through the small opening.

Footfalls echoed through my ears as they moved up the steps and down the long hall to the attic. I closed the alcove door and pushed against the cypress chest. The wooden floors creaking against the footfalls I scurried towards the alcove window as the door opened.

Auntie

The attic door opened, and my aunt's narrowed eyes turned into sharp blades that cut me into pieces. I struggled to maintain my breathing and slow my heart-rate so as not to give away my adventure.

She sneered, "They're gone. Go to your room."

Without hesitation I scampered past her and to my room. I didn't want anything to do with anyone in my horrible family. My grandmother had proven as dreadful as my aunt. I was a "secret". Their dark child who had no place in the family.

My back against the mattress of my bed I thought back to the day Noela was killed. I cried for her, not for my cousin or his boyfriend who killed her, but for her. I adored her. How could this woman not shed a real tear for her husband? A man she'd spent her life with, had a child with.

She was cold, her words hollow, even the tears she dropped for the police were an act. My grandma hadn't seen a thing but in her voice I heard her skepticism. If my aunt hadn't murdered him herself, she didn't lift a finger to stop it.

His death was later ruled accidental. They believed her story. Malery found a way to blame me when he came home for Christmas and his daddy's funeral. He took that doll of his and poked a needle between its eyes. "I know somehow you did this," he seethed, poking the needle further in until only the round ball on the end could be seen.

I refused to believe. If I did I'd have felt the sharp pain radiating through my forehead. *Voodoo isn't real, voodoo isn't real,* I chanted silently. No, I wouldn't give him the pleasure. On the other hand, I was glad to see somebody truly mourned the man's death since even his wife didn't. If I admitted it, I felt guilty as if I'd pushed him myself. My brain replayed the scene so many times I knew I hadn't done it and couldn't say who did or maybe it was an awful accident. A part of me didn't believe that.

The rift between my grandmother and aunt lengthened. Stretched like a rubber band. I couldn't stand to be in the room with them. They knew what he did as they talked silently with facial expressions. Grandma's tight lips and narrowed eyes saying, "Told you that man was no good."

My aunt simmering, her oval face drooping like a worn beanbag, new lines forming around her eyes as if saying, 'Piece of shit. I warned him, but if it wasn't for that girl.'

Outside under the tree was peaceful. The glassy water mirrored the stories of the bayou yet held them captive. Dangling branches swayed overhead dripping in Spanish moss. Its trunk wrinkled with time, worn with age. Each crease and line holding onto a secret it whispered to the air. I listened with my head nestled in the bulky roots of the large cypress, murmurs filled the air, so many voices speaking at once they were impossible to discern.

I once had a family that loved me but my memories of them were so vague. When I closed my eyes I saw Momma's ebony face so much lighter than I remember only years earlier. The hours she spent outside, running along the beach, primping her flower garden, darkened her skin. Her full lips kissed my cheek and I felt safe wrapped in her arms.

Her laughter, mixed with my father's, lit up my world. I didn't know cruelty existed. That I had family deep, deep in the bayou. My roots thick and deep as the cypress. Their lineage old as the cypress. I was merely a child caught in a web of deceit and hate.

My mind wasn't mature enough yet to understand how deep my aunt's hate for me swelled but I was beginning to understand. I clasped the locket around my neck and closed my eyes. Behind my lids I saw the grand house with shining floors and fixtures, horses and carriages, blossoming dresses and shiny shoes. Parasols and colored people sweeping palm branches to keep the white people cool in the hot, sticky, summer air.

Those days had passed, people of the town didn't care and paid no mind to the color of my skin or the tight curls on my head. Why then did my uncle, Malery, and especially my aunt, loathe each breath I took and the ground I walked on? It niggled at my brain, so close, yet distant enough I couldn't capture it.

Grandma, my betrayer, confused my emotions further with her next move.

Part 2
Death
Becomes Me

Initiation

After the holidays my grandmother abruptly deposited me at Ella Louise School for Girls. The reason didn't matter, not that I knew what it was. I was temporarily free from the shackles of White Oak.

My roommate, Lissa, helped me carry my luggage up the Y-shaped staircase that spiraled and came full circle for each of the three levels to our room.

Lissa's vibrant attitude lit up the room. With her board-straight black hair, shining white teeth behind moist pink lips, high cheek bones, and silky brown almond eyes, she was beautiful.

Robin, my other roommate, was tall, gangly, with ginger waves, and freckled, pale white skin that contrasted her large round brown eyes. Not nearly the shining star Lissa was but she was beautiful in an awkward way.

They sat at the foot of my bed talking as I unpacked.

Lissa didn't ever really stop talking. She filled me in on classes and the teachers. What to expect and classes to never be late too. Robin offered small hints here and there but not much. Not that she had a chance to say anything. Lissa's voice filled the airwaves in the room.

My bed and chest of drawers were nearest the door. Lissa's closest to the window and Robin's across from us.

The room was pleasant with cream walls and light green comforters and curtains. The window was large with an alcove.

I arrived mid-afternoon on a Saturday so, after unpacking, it was time for dinner.

The butterflies in my belly jumped around so much from the adrenaline rush of being away from White Oak and my dysfunctional family I didn't have any appetite. Some of the butterflies were also due to making friends and being part of a group. I was embarking on a brand-new chapter in my life and it was exhilarating as much as it was frightening.

I moved the food around my plate as I took in the grand cafeteria with its wainscoting and massive chandeliers. The floors shone brighter than a sailor's dress shoe. It was like a ballroom. I imagined Cinderella floating around the floor in her poufy blue dress with Prince Charming.

My mind a million miles away, I didn't notice the girl standing at the end of the table glaring at me.

She cleared her throat and said in a deep voice, "Hey, new girl."

I met her gaze but didn't respond. She was at least a couple years older than me. Her lips weren't more than a pencil line across her face and barely moved as she spoke. "Don't be late." She shoved a folded paper at me then walked off, taking a seat with three other girls. One with thick, blond waves and deep blue pools for eyes, glanced at me and winked.

I unfolded the paper and was overcome with a vision. A small stream of light from the moon shone across the dusty air and a person, I couldn't tell whether female or male, fell forward. Its motion halted as it tripped and fell over something, a railing maybe. A squishing sound was simultaneous with a distorted scream. Like my other visions, I watched death happen but was unable to see a face and, without more details, was helpless in understanding who or why I saw it.

I dropped the paper and squeezed my eyes closed and when I reopened them the image changed. It was a hand-drawn map of the school grounds and said 'midnight tonight' with an X outside the building's walls. I let out a breath and regained composure.

Lissa, sitting across from me, leaned over expectantly. Her eyes shifting from the paper to me.

"What is this?" I asked instead of spilling my crazy vision. I'd never told anyone about them but Miss. Dresdan knew. She said I was touched. *But why did I always see death?*

Lissa opened up with, "Initiation. You have to do it!"

Robin interjected, "It's a social status thing. If you don't do it you're an outcast and that's hard in a boarding school where you spend every second with those who shun you."

I opened my mouth to speak but before I got the words out Lissa said, "You'll become a Scrap."

"A Scrap?" I asked meekly.

Robin clung to each of Lissa's words with me.

"You see those tables in the corner by the exit?"

I nodded. Sitting at them was what looked like a group of about fifteen girls having a good time as they leaned in and talked, leaned out and laughed as one girl balanced a Brussels sprout on her nose.

"They're Scraps. Either they didn't go to initiation or failed it. Either way, they are Scraps as long as they attend Ella Louise," Lissa said in one breath.

Robin confirmed with a head nod.

"What about everyone else?"

"Well," Lissa began. "They all passed initiation."

I shoved a small bite of chicken in my mouth to avoid conversation. I wanted to be part of a group. To have friends. So it seemed I had no choice but to do it.

Lissa's eyes opened wide. "I see the wheels in your mind spinning. See the girls by the food line? They're the jocks and don't care about anything but sports and getting scholarships. Most of them don't come from money. The girls behind them are nerds. One of them will make valedictorian. If you need a paper, that's the group. Most of them will go to

Ivy League Colleges and become doctors and lawyers. The girls in front of us are the hoes."

What was a hoe besides a gardening tool in the shed? Robin must have picked up on my confusion of the word and followed up with, "Girls that have sex with all the boys from Landsom Academy for Boys across the woods and over the river from here."

My mind immediately went backwards to the night Noela died when I saw Malery having sex with another boy in the woods and how that boy killed my only friend. I'm sure I shuddered visibly. "They all passed initiation?"

Lissa and Robin nodded.

"You passed too?"

They nodded again.

How bad could it be if at least three quarters of everyone made it? "What can you tell me about it?"

Lissa's eyes narrowed into slits. "Nothing. We're sworn to secrecy and you will be too."

We finished eating and rushed back to our room. Lissa shoved a chair under the doorknob. "What I'm going to show you is top secret. Only Robin knows. Turn around and close your eyes."

I glanced at Robin who shrugged and nodded confirmation that we should follow Lissa's orders.

I listened intently but heard only a small squeak before Lissa spoke again.

"Turn around, open your eyes."

We did. In her hand was a small tin. "My dad owns Mintech and he gives me this stuff." She pulled a jeweled barrette out of the tin and a matching jeweled ring.

"This is a receiver so we can hear everything and this," she threaded her finger into the ring, "is a transmitter so you can speak to us."

She slid the barrette into my hair, a smidge above my ear. "You have a head of hair, you know that?"

I giggled. "It's pretty wild."

"It's pretty," Robin added as she took the ring off Lissa's finger and slipped it on mine. "You might be the prettiest girl here so watch out for Greta. She's not as angelic as she looks."

"Greta?" I asked in confusion.

"The blond that is the look of perfection as if cast from a mold."

"Oh, yeah. She was sitting--"

Lissa cut me off. "We can't tell you what's going to happen but we can tell you to watch your back, stay strong. Greta smells fear. Don't let her smell yours and whatever you do don't be obvious with the stuff I gave you."

My words of warning. I thought of them as I left Lissa and Robin who I knew would be listening in all night. The only way for me to hear them was the ring. They worked like a phone and had one of their own.

Ghosts and Haunts

Two other girls stood outside the courtyard, waiting. Both looked nervous as one rocked on her heels and the other bit her nails.

"Hi," I offered. *Stay strong,* I reminded myself. *It couldn't be worse or scarier than the attic could it?*

The girl biting her nails replied nervously, "Hi. I'm Tymara."

I nodded and silence persisted. One minute turned into many, or so it seemed, until three girls in cloaks with hoods covering their heads walked towards us, hands behind their backs. I couldn't see their faces as their hoods made long shadows across them in the darkness.

When they got to us they brought their hands out, each with a gunny sack.

"Scream and you're done," one of the cloaked girls said in a deep voice. It sounded like the one who dropped off the note but I wasn't sure.

They dropped the gunny sacks over our heads and another spoke, her voice higher pitched:"You can't see where you're going but we'll take them off when we get there."

The sacks had small holes between the threads allowing me to see glimpses; bare trees, lots of them, and no path. The ground was littered with winter leaves that crunched beneath our feet. Using my hearing I listened intently making out the distinct sound of rushing water. The river. Lissa, no Robin mentioned it earlier. The hoes came this way to meet boys and have sex.

"Stop," the deeper-voiced girl announced.

Soon the sacks came off and the three cloaked girls moved behind the blond one who was also wearing a cloak but had her hood down.

Greta I guessed, as she looked like a porcelain doll. Enough blush her cheeks were pink against her fair skin and her pools of blue were round and evenly set.

Greta spoke, "New girls. You haven't earned the right to your name yet but if you complete the challenges tonight you will. If not..." She paused for dramatic effect. "If at any time tonight you tuck your tail between your legs and run you will become a Scrap and that is all you will ever be. A Scrap left for the dogs." She studied us with long glances as she strolled in front of us. Greta stopped in front of Tymara. "You must stop that. Take your fingers out of your mouth. Are you five?"

Tymara immediately drew her hands away and put them behind her back.

The three girls behind Greta stood still as if frozen in place. Trees and lightning bugs silhouetted them.

"Are you retarded?" Greta asked the other girl as she rocked nervously. The girl stopped on command.

I remembered Lissa's words not to show fear so I held my chest out, back straight and shoulders square, as Greta stopped in front of me. She tilted her head, full blond waves falling over her chest. "Hmm... you show promise. Must be old," she stretched out the word, "money."

The way she said it I wondered if she knew my grandmother. My family was old money but I was the forbidden, hidden child. How did I know how to act in such situations? I lacked the training, galas, and schooling others didn't.

Greta continued her stroll with her porcelain hands adorned with manicured nails behind her back. "This school was purchased nearly 150 years ago. Anybody who's anybody came here to learn the proper training a Southern Lady requires. Before that it was a plantation named Ella Louise after the owner's wife. Her beauty was known throughout Louisiana and among other southern plantation owners. He loved her so much he bought this beautiful property for her and designed her dream house which we sleep and eat in now."

She paused for a second and glanced us. "The slave master found her one afternoon having intimate relations with a slave." Her voice became very animated. "She claimed he raped her and everyone believed it."

Pausing in front of me she stared me in the eye. "Black people were nothing. Livestock." I guessed that was a personal hit on me but I'd heard worse from Malery. "The owner was so heartbroken and enraged that night he burned the slave's quarters down with him and his family inside."

The girl beside me rocked backwards on her heel, that's all it took for Greta to catch it and throw her the evil eye.

She didn't pause a beat as she continued. "The next night the owner choked on a worm in his dinner wine. He died. What he didn't know when he burned the slave's quarters was that he was a voodoo practitioner like many other slaves in these parts. He'd cursed him in his death of flames. Nine months later his wife died giving birth to a black baby."

Her blue pools fixated on me. I was the mixed, forbidden child here. "No one knows what happened to the baby. Some people say other slaves took it as their own, others say it was taken through the underground railroad to the north. The house was sold years later and became the fine Institute we are part of today." They'd warned me about her. 'Pretty as a doll, mean as a rattlesnake,' had been Lissa's words. She didn't look so mean, but a dark, cruel soul came in all types of packages. Grandma's betrayal hurt, stung like a swat across my back. Greta couldn't hurt that badly.

Greta waved an arm and the girls behind her turned around, then again, facing us they held metal chalices in their hands.

"Your first test is to drink from the chalice. You can't leave a drop at the bottom. One of them has a worm. If you get that one you must eat it."

The hooded girls walked towards us, each with a metal chalice as Greta spoke again, "Which one of you will get the wriggling worm tonight? Who dares drink?"

She studied our faces, while each of us grabbed a chalice. It was this moment I wished my vision extended to seeing something besides death. *Was there a way to control it?* Pushing all my focus towards the chalice I attempted to *see* with my vision and was dismayed when I couldn't.

"Whoever has the worm must eat it," she seethed as a mischievous smile played across her face.

On her count we lifted the chalices and drank. Tymara gagged and spit. The worm flew from her mouth, hitting one of the cloaked girls in the face. It slid down her cheek and dropped to the ground. A chuckle rose up from somewhere buried deep inside and I laughed out loud.

Greta didn't like that none. "Pick up that worm," she ordered one of the cloaked girls and sauntered towards me. "You think that's funny?"

I laughed harder and, like laughter does, it became contagious as the Rocker stifled a chuckle.

"You can eat it then!"

The cloaked girl brought it closer, dangling it in my face. All eyes were on me. I accepted the challenge. *Show no fear.*

She rubbed it across my nose and with a gulp I sunk my teeth into it. What I never told anyone about that worm was that it was a candy worm; a gummy. I didn't let on as I chewed and swallowed that worm with a look of disgust. Tymara and the Rocker stared at me, mouths dropped open and eyes widened.

It was that challenge that I think set the tone for Greta and me. She respected that I didn't call her bluff and spill that it was only a candy but she never got over that I laughed.

Since Tymara didn't pass the challenge she dismissed her, placing a joker's hat on her head. Each of its peaks red, green and blue. "You are a Scrap and must hang out in the Scrap pile with the other Scraps. This hat must be worn for the next week, everywhere but in class. Don't let me catch you with it off. Now, leave us SCRAP."

Water welled in the corners of Tymara's eyes as Greta dropped that hat on her head. It was cruel. I gulped but kept my stance. I wouldn't show fear or sadness. I stayed strong even though my heart wanted to scream at Greta for being so mean.

"The next part of the challenge you will spend the night here. The spot you stand is where the slave's quarters were. He and the slave owner have been seen wandering the woods searching for Ella Louise. But no one has ever seen her."

Greta backed away then and she and the three girls disappeared into the rising fog. I listened as their footsteps carried them away.

With Tymara gone there was just the two of us. Nothing was there but grass although she insisted the little house had sat there. I think she just found a spot and called it. In the woods surrounded by the stars and silence of winter.

"This is bullshit!" the Rocker said as she pulled her coat around her chest to keep the cold at bay.

"It's not so bad," I answered, lowering myself to the ground, and watched the fog roll in.

She sat across from me. "Yes, it is, even the ground is wet."

"Leave. I'll stay here alone." I truly didn't want to be out there alone but I was used to the fog and nothingness. White Oak was surrounded by water and woods.

I lowered my head and brought my hand to my mouth and whispered, "Still with me?"

Robin and Lissa's voices came through. "Of course."

Lissa dominated the conversation. "It's not over. Don't fall asleep. Keep your eyes peeled."

I couldn't see anything through the fog. It was thickening each second. But I could see with my ears. "What's your name?"

"Not Scrap. You're brave. What you did with the worm, that was funny."

"I'm Debbie."

She scooted closer. "Johnie."

"That's an odd name for a girl?"

"Short for Johanna. My brother couldn't say it right when I was born so he called me Johnie. It stuck." She paused then got her thought out, "Do you think that story is true?"

I kept my hand rested by my chin. "I don't know."

Lissa's voice came through, "It is, most of it anyways. The owner's official death record said he choked on a worm and the wife died in child birth. The part about the slave I could never confirm."

"I think they made it up to scare us," Johnie offered.

Blurry flashes of light moved through the misty woods, followed by the sounds of mushy footsteps. Johnie scooted closer to me. "You think that's them? You know. Trying to scare us?"

"Sure, probably," I guessed. The cold creeping through my flannel pajamas.

The rolling fog through the bare trees made the night unnerving as we sat close to one another for warmth. Our breath visible in the air. We talked to fill the airspace with sound so we didn't feel so alone and scared.

I traced the way back to the school in my mind. Between the threads in the gunny sack I'd seen enough I thought maybe I could find my way back. I noted my surroundings; a tree withered and bent like a teapot. The trees were all so tall and thin it was hard to decipher one from another except the teapot. The flow of water from the river rushed through my ears.

"You can't stay there," Lissa said through the barrette. "They won't stay out there long in this cold. When they come back you and Johnie need to leave. There's a shed not far. Follow the river and you'll find it.

"OK," I whispered. "You'll let us know."

"Of course," Robin's voice came through.

"Who are you talking to?" Johnie asked, one eyebrow raised.

Ignoring her question, I lifted myself from the ground with the urge to dust off the dirt, only my wet bottoms clung to my butt. I offered my hands to Johnie and she grabbed them, accepting my assistance.

We walked in circles, talking to stay warm. Movement helped stave off the cold but I was still freezing and considered returning back to the school and living as a Scrap. I couldn't do that. I had the chance to be part of something. To make friends. As long as I moved I'd be OK. I was stupid not to bring my coat.

Thirty minutes or so passed before Lissa confirmed the four girls had returned. "Let's go. I'm freezing and I think I heard someone say something earlier about some buildings out here, like sheds or something. Somewhere at least we can be dry."

"Sounds like a plan. The sticks and ground are too moist with mist to even start a fire." She scratched her head. "I was an Adventure Scout. It was a badge I earned."

I didn't bother to ask what an Adventure Scout was. Assumed it was one of those things I was forbidden from doing. One of those things people did to learn, socialize, and make connections.

"My coat is big enough for the both of us." She pulled an arm out and offered it to me.

I shook my head. "It would slow us down. Do you hear the river?"

She nodded.

"We should follow it," I suggested, remembering Lissa's words.

Sound waves carried the river closer with each step until it sounded like we were in the middle of it. Carefully navigating the fog, we found the river's edge and froze when we heard a distinct squish of a boot in the mushy earth.

Follow the River

Our eyes round and wide, Johnie and I stared at each other. The blanket of fog thick, I couldn't disseminate from where the squishing originated. Footfalls surrounded us, ran past us and kept going until we didn't hear them anymore.

"It's them," Johnie whispered, meaning Greta and gang, but was it? I wasn't so sure.

"They're still in their rooms. I swear not one of them has left," Lissa said in my ear. The fear residing in my gut expanded that moment and my heart dropped to my feet. A dragging sound neared us. I squatted and tugged Johnie's leg.

Immediately she dropped, our hearts thumping like wild horses. She pressed her lips against my ear, "The fog hides us but someone is there. We need to run."

Drag, drag… shuffle. It was getting closer. There was only time to react. "If we run," I pointed to my left, "that way we'll be moving away from it." I was about ninety-five percent sure. That was good enough.

In her hand was a large rock. She pushed it towards me in offering. I wasted no time in clutching it. Whatever was in the woods with us, human or beast, it would at least serve some amount of self-defense. In her own hand she clutched one of similar size.

The adrenaline rushing through my veins, I was suddenly warm and my sweat gathered over the rock in my hand. I pushed up a finger, then another, and a third and we were on our feet, moving forward. I barely felt each foot hit the ground as one step then another sunk into the wet dirt.

The rushing water steady in my ears. Every breath I drew loud as a train. The blood pumped through my extremities as if a raging fire, then through the fog a form appeared. I nearly ran into it as I skidded to a stop.

The stars absent from the sky and a moist envelope sealed around me, I barely made out that it was Johnie. No more than a few inches taller than me with short, dark hair sticking to her neck she stretched an arm in front of her. An orangey-yellow light scarcely visible wasn't more than a few feet in front of us.

I reached for her hand and we scooted closer. I'd felt plenty of fear that night but that glow stirred something else in me -- the warm, tingly feeling of death. I took a step forward, shoving death aside.

She shook her head. "No. Whatever's in there is bad."

Letting go of her hand I moved forward alone. Cautiously, I lowered each foot to avoid making any sound until I stood to the side of the open window and peered into a cabin. It definitely wasn't the shed. Flames glowed from a fireplace. It was inviting, but nowhere did I see a person.

A blood-curdling shriek chilled my already freezing bones into ice cubes that shattered as I turned around.

My eyes making contact with a man, his eyes the only distinguishing characteristic; blue with cloudy shadows that danced across them. The light through the window shone on an object in his hand. A blade, sharp, blood dropped from the tip. *Drop...drop...* Panic seized me, terror dug its claws into my legs and climbed up my body. I opened my mouth to scream when a thwack rumbled and he dropped.

A second thwack, no, it was softer, mushier. Mimicking the sound of a squishing body but on a grander scale thudded as the body landed on a spike that went through his chest. It poked through his back to the ground, legs falling one direction and his head dropping forward only inches from my feet. My vision at dinner that played out on the paper. If I wasn't the grim reaper, then I was his unwilling helper. I side-stepped and reminded myself to breathe.

Johnie dashed to my side. "Debbie," she muttered through short breaths. "I saw it. I saw it. That was a gun in his hand. He was going to kill you."

I met her wild gaze, eyes shifting back and forth in their sockets. I swallowed. "He's dead isn't he?"

She nodded. "I think so." Suddenly she shuddered and covered her face with her hands. "I did that. I did that. I did that!" Each time she said it her voice grew louder and trembled worse.

"It's OK. It's OK," I reassured her without looking at the dead man near my feet. It wasn't OK. Her body shook so badly I had to say something to calm her. I moved around the side of him and concentrated only on his hands, searching for the gun. His hand lay in an awkward position at his side. In his hand was a gun. I studied it harder, sure it had been a knife. It transformed before my eyes.

I blinked several times, trying to focus on the object that kept changing. *Gun... knife... gun... knife.* The bizarre object was like nothing I'd ever seen. It didn't know what it was but I knew my *touch* was messing with me.

Johnie rocked on her feet, back and forth. Forgetting the strange object I took her hand. "We need to leave." We couldn't hang around. Truth be told, I didn't know what to do, but Johnie was in such a state I only thought to get her back to the school.

She nodded, her eyes far away as if in a dream. With an arm around her shoulders we walked towards the school, at least the direction I thought the school should be.

Johnie mumbled under her breath, "I'd rather be a Scrap. I knew, I saw. I saw. I always see..."

I halted. "What do you mean you see?"

Her crazed eyes looked square into mine. "I see things. The gun. I didn't see it through the fog but earlier in my mind. It shows me things. Stuff I don't want to see."

A set up. Someone knew I was *touched,* that I was *touched with sight* and this whole thing was to get me to admit it. I halted. "If I go back, that man will still be there?"

A mix of confusion and sadness crossed her face. "Where would he go? I kill...ed him." A flood of tears drained from her eyes. "I killed him." Snot fled from her nose as she wiped it with her arm.

This wasn't an act. The fear and desperation in her were real. There was no option but to get her back to the house, but we'd come so far I wasn't sure how to get there. We wandered until the gold covered the sky burning some of the fog away. Johnie became more lucid with each step. The walking kept us both sane.

Through the leafless trees, the large house with its mountains and valleys were visible. Lissa and Robin's voices rang into my ear with a parade of questions. "I'll tell you soon," I whispered.

I took the barrette out of my hair and the ring off my finger and squeezed them in the palm of my hand to muffle the sound. "Johnie, look at me."

She lifted her head from the spot on the ground she'd been concentrating on.

"Whatever happened out there, it didn't happen. We can't tell a soul about this night. We're tired and need sleep and that's it. Got it?" I said in a firm voice. I didn't like hiding it but it was self-defense like when I killed Noela's attacker. I didn't mean to. I only wanted him to let go of her.

"I got it," her voice gaining clarity and strength. "I'm sorry. You must think... we should go back. Maybe it didn't happen the way we think?"

I nodded. "No, we go back to the school," I insisted.

When we reached the school, Greta stood with arms across her chest and disdain painted on her porcelain face. "You girls look a mess. Did you roll in the dirt all night?"

Tired and wanting nothing more than a shower, we walked past her.

"Where do you think you're going and where is Sam?"

Spies

reta didn't like that we snubbed her but we finished the challenge, stayed out all night. Johnie's room was across the hall.

The second I entered mine I was met with expectant faces and a slew of questions. Lissa and Robin met me at the door and took up residence on the edge of my bed as I recalled the night's events. They'd fallen asleep about three in the morning and knew nothing about what we did. I filled them in on the rest and admitted we never found the shed but wandered back on our own as dawn's light peeked over the horizon.

The night was surreal, as if it hadn't happened, yet I was covered in dirt that said it did. I still didn't know one thing: "Who is Sam?"

Robin and Lissa glanced at each other then me, "That's Greta's friend. The one who served you the initiation invitation."

I nodded and opened my chest of drawers. It was time for a shower and sleep. With my clothes and shower kit in hand I padded to the door, barely able to hold myself up from exhaustion.

Robin spoke, "You can't leave yet, leaving us hanging. What about Sam?"

I shrugged my shoulders that drooped like boiled spaghetti. "She went to find us this morning but didn't come back with us. We weren't at the spot. I'm sure she's back now."

The warm water over my head was like a dream. Dirt ran from my extremities and head. I watched as it swirled down the drain. I crossed my fingers, hoping Sam wasn't late because she'd found the body. No, she couldn't, we were too far off the path. Nowhere near the spot they left us.

In a fresh, clean, sweat suit I entered the bedroom, ready to lay down and sleep the day away. Robin and Lissa were gone which meant no one was there to talk and keep me awake. My eyelids snapped shut when my body hit the soft bed.

A dreamless sleep was abruptly disturbed by a commotion in the hallway. Feet running, long, distorted voices and the creak of the bedroom door opening.

"Get up, Debbie," Lissa's voice clarified as she shook me fully awake.

With drowsy eyes I blinked as she came into focus. "What's going on?"

Lissa's eyes wide and feral, her face warped with terror, words flew from her mouth without a single breath, "Sam is missing. When she didn't come for breakfast Ms. Timble, the dean, asked Greta where she was and Greta told her she wasn't in bed when she woke up. Thought she went for a morning run."

Those words woke me, I grabbed her shoulders. *Did she find the body?* No, she'd be back, panicked and scared. *Was she the body?* I remembered how the weapon kept changing, morphing from a gun to a knife. Maybe there was no weapon at all and we'd killed her. "I'm sure she's fine."

"How? How are you sure? She's not back. Sam has been at this school four years, since she was our age, she knows the grounds. She can find her way back from anywhere." Her feral eyes turned desperate.

At that moment Robin entered, closed the door behind her. Eyes fixated on us as she nervously twisted her hands.

I thought of the shriek. I'd thought it was Johnie but maybe it wasn't. The entire episode was more dreamlike than reality. At that moment I wasn't even sure we'd seen what we'd seen. Did what we did. "It was just us last night. You heard everything. You know what happened. Nothing. Maybe she's still searching for us. She was sent to retrieve us but we found our way back. Walking is what kept us from freezing. I'm sure she'll be back soon."

Sam never showed and a search team was sent to look for her. *How deep into the wilderness surrounding the school had we gone?*

Mixed emotions of anxiety and sorrow filled the school that day. It was quiet and whispers carried in the halls that Greta was responsible. She never faltered in the schedule and everyone knew it was an initiation night. When Greta entered a room it fell silent.

When the pressure was more than Greta could bear she pulled Johnie and me aside, guiding us into an empty broom closet. She pulled the chain light, illuminating the darkness. Cleaning supplies and a wringer that reeked of bleach left little room for the three of us.

"You tell me what happened last night," Greta said in a demanding tone, resting a hand on each of our arms. Her face distorted. She quickly pulled her hand away from my arm.

"We don't know. Nothing happened last night," Johnie said in a shaky voice.

I sucked down the dread resting at the edge of my throat. "We walked. You left us in the cold all night. We walked to stay warm, hoping to find at least a dry shed or something but we didn't and we *never* saw Sam."

Greta's round eyes narrowed into slits. "If she isn't found by the search team we're going out there and finding her tonight."

Sam didn't come back and the team found nothing, abandoning their search when the sun took its leave. Armed with flashlights, we ran into the night.

I remembered to wear a coat and the cold wasn't so bad. The fog rolled in, not as bad as the previous night. We had clear vision for about five to six feet in front of us.

Once we made it to the place Greta left us -- the slaves' quarters -- she grabbed Johnie's hand. Johnie glanced at her with disdain and wiggled her hand away. Greta ignored it. "You will show me your exact steps last night."

The air was so thick with moisture the previous night I couldn't remember. Nothing was familiar except the teapot tree. "We heard the river and walked towards it."

"Sam," Greta called in desperation. "Call for her," she demanded as we searched.

The beams from our flashlights flooded the area around us as we walked, attempting to retrace our steps. Once we reached the river, other than the sound of its whoosh, the area wasn't familiar at all, although I guessed that's because we couldn't really see it. It had been a blurry haze at best.

"If the search team didn't find her what makes you think we will?" I asked, watching Greta shine her flashlight on the ground as if in search of something specific like a lost earring.

"Because they didn't have you to guide them," she seethed.

Johnie jumped to our defense, "We told you we didn't see or hear anything, at least nothing but our own fear."

Greta lifted the flashlight into Johnie's face forcing Johnie to squint her eyes and look away. "Don't back-talk me. I'm older and wiser in life than you. Didn't your parents teach you any manners?!"

"Your parents didn't or you wouldn't have covered our heads in gunny sacks so we couldn't find our way back and left us in the freezing night alone!" I jumped down Greta's throat, expecting the gleam of her flashlight I shifted mine first, right into her eyes. "Hurts doesn't it. Don't ever do that again!"

As if expecting it she shifted her gaze away. "You are a feisty one, gutsy."

Those words brought on a case of déjà vu. Malery saying something similar, somewhere along my dismal path of life.

"There," Greta pointed with the flashlight towards sinking footprints in the mushy ground.

We followed her and the footprints until they disappeared. She shone the flashlight in circles on the ground. "Where did they go?"

Instinctively, I knew we were close to the cabin. I couldn't see the orangey-yellow glow of the fireplace, but of course I wouldn't. We killed its occupant and the fire, without more wood, would die. "I think we took a left here away from the river to find our way back to the school."

She touched Johnie's hand again. "Are you sure?"

Johnie whipped her hand away again. "No, it was dark and foggy. None of this even looks familiar."

Greta took a couple steps forward, her face inches from mine. "You're lying. We move forward."

I straightened my back and squared my shoulders. "Like she said, it was hard to see, but I'm sure we went left here." I brought my hand to her face and she jumped backwards out of my reach. I didn't know what was up with her touching thing but she sure didn't want her skin to meet mine. Maybe she was a germaphobe. I'd heard about it or read it.

Edges of familiarity, ghosts of the previous night entered my awareness as we neared what I was sure was where we found the cabin.

Greta's light panned the ground, halted only by the cabin. Johnie swallowed as her eyes shifted nervously searching for the body. The one we were sure was there. Only it wasn't.

I glanced at her, our eyes meeting and in silent words, spoken only through our eyes, told her to remain calm.

Greta neared Johnie and lifted her hand. In a sudden outburst Johnie wailed, "Stop touching me!"

Taken aback, Greta recoiled. "Well I never..." Disgust and surprise crisscrossed her face. "Fine!"

I stepped forward towards Greta, my eyes directed to her but with my peripheral vision and other senses I searched for any clue that last night happened. "I told you we took a left back there by the river."

Greta took a step backwards then turned on her heel and headed towards the door to the cabin.

"What are you doing?" Johnie asked, nervous anxiety evident in her voice.

Greta flipped her hair behind her shoulder. "Tch... I'm going in. What does it look like I'm doing?"

Find Sam

*J*ohnie and I apprehensively followed Greta inside the cabin. *What if we hadn't killed the person but injured him and he crawled back into the cabin and died inside it?* I fully expected to see a bloody body sprawled on the floor. Its arm reaching for a couch or bed as it took its final breath.

I shone my flashlight on the ground, seeking a bloodied trail, but there was none. Not even the tell-tale drag of a body across the dirt. I sucked in a deep breath before entering. It was empty. Not a body, not a person, just us.

The cabin was small, not meant for daily living. The fireplace cold and absent of flames. It was chilly and dark, our flashlights the only thing that brightened it up. There wasn't much to see, a small table and chairs, a futon and a couple cabinets over a kitchenette the size of a bathroom closet. The restroom itself lacked a shower or tub.

Unsatisfied, but with no more leads, we vacated the cabin and headed back to the school empty-handed. Sam's whereabouts remained a mystery. The days turned into weeks and still no Sam. Greta's status waned as some of the girls blamed her, others sided with her.

Tymara caught me after class one day. As a Scrap she sided with the Scraps who all blamed Greta. "What happened that night? You know, after I left?" Her eyes staring at a spot on the wall, she wouldn't even make eye contact with me.

"Nothing. We wandered in the cold to stay warm until the sun came up," I answered.

She stuck a hand in her mouth and spoke but the words came out slurred, "So Greta is innocent?" It took my brain a few seconds to piece the words together.

I cleared my throat. "I didn't say that. If it wasn't for her we wouldn't have been out there and Sam wouldn't have come looking to meet us and bring us back to the school."

Pulling the hand from her mouth and shifting her eyes from the interesting spot on the wall to meet mine she said, "You're right," then shuffled towards the door.

I opened my mouth to speak before she left, "You're not a Scrap. There are no Scraps. You have a name, a beautiful one. Don't give Greta the power, seize it from her."

One side of her mouth lifted in a smile as my words sunk in. "You're right." I knew that. I'd given Malery and my aunt power for years. No more would anyone hold it over me. I had broken free. That was the humble beginning of the Scrap Uprising.

Johnie and I formed a bond through our experience. We were both *touched.* That night in the woods she had seen something different than me. A man in a ski mask with a gun. She threw the rock into his head and he dropped, falling onto an object that impaled him. Neither of us pieced together the shriek, each thinking it was the other. We knew it was neither, but Sam. It was Sam, something bad happened to her. We both knew it and each day the anxiety grew.

We shared our visions and how our *touch* worked. Lissa and Robin were great and we were close but Johnie and I were nearly inseparable. She mostly had visions after touching objects. That night when she took the chalice she saw someone fall on a spike. For me it didn't work that way. The first time I awoke from my sleep and didn't even know the man. In the woods with Noela, I hadn't touched anything and with Malery when he poked the doll I saw someone's fiery death.

It helped to talk with someone else who could relate but neither of us knew why we always saw death. It haunted us our entire lives. Through our discussions I realized the man we killed in the woods was the same man who broke into White Oak the night I was left alone. The gunman with the ski mask had appeared in her visions before. She figured her mind put his face on death since she always watched him die. For me the man with the knife wasn't always there, usually I saw a blurry face.

Spring break arrived. I had no desire to go home. Most of the girls did, but no one came for me. I hadn't reminded Grandma when break was and she'd most likely forgot. I also avoided speaking with her. It was easy here to forestall the inevitable confrontation with Grandma and White Oak.

Johnie stayed on too. Her mother recently remarried and was honeymooning overseas. It was perfect. Our overactive imaginations wanted to know more about the story Greta told. We figured the house had to hold the secrets so we sneaked to the third floor library. It was off limits. Ms. Timble claimed it was under construction.

We'd never seen anyone go up there, not workers, staff, not even the librarians. With precise articulation we planned it. Learned where the dean kept the keys to every room. I sneaked in while Johnie stood guard. No one would miss a key to a room never visited. Giggling like school children we climbed the steps. The large tear-drop door loomed as I fit in the key I'd borrowed.

As the metal bolts rolled into place the door clicked and I pushed. It was much heavier than I expected but Johnie helped and the door opened into a large room filled with books and old furniture. The sun spilled through the window making it airy even with the dark burgundy walls. Dust tickled our noses as we raced from one end to the next.

These were not library books but blueprints of the home's design and ledgers. It was shaped like a square. In the middle was a courtyard and in each of the four corners a third floor with a castle tower peak. The third floor of the library was in one of the peaks. The roof came to a point. Inside the ceiling was a rounded reverse dome with a mural.

A painting of the original owner and his wife -- Damen and Ella Louise Hartley -- hung from one of the walls. She was beautiful with long, full, blond hair, bright blue round eyes, and a delicate face with a heart-shaped chin. Her lips parted in a confident smile. His dark hair and rugged features a contrast to her. His looks grew on me as he watched from the painting and he became more handsome by the second.

There were detailed ledgers accounting for revenue, slaves, purchases, investments. Most didn't make much sense to two pre-teen girls from the 1990s. It was fascinating, even if every ledger was a list of numbers and words without meaning.

"Look!" Johnie hollered as she scampered to me.

She shoved a yellowed paper into my face. I studied it. A copy of the owner's death certificate. The cause of death was listed as choking.

"Turn the page. There's more."

The next page was a coroner's report, or the equivalent for the late 1850s, and explained a worm was found in his throat and considered the reason he choked. "It's true." I lowered the paper and rested my back against the wall.

"It is. Did you find anything?"

"Slave records. They were very meticulous listing each purchase and sale, the price and even the slaves' names, every death and birth." I handed her one of the ledgers.

"This is amazing! I feel like I stepped into a time capsule." She dropped to the floor beside me. "Do you think the wife's baby is in here? I mean... if that part of the story is true."

"I don't know. I haven't found anything about a fire but I do find the owner to be contagiously attractive in a dark, rugged way."

She glanced at the picture on the wall as if she hadn't yet noticed it and tilted her head. "Yeah, he's brooding like a vampire or something."

The sun lowered in the sky, lavenders and reds filled the landscape. Johnie jumped up, her eyes wild. "Dinner! We have to go before they look for us!"

I grabbed several ledgers I hadn't had the chance yet to search and she grabbed a few more and we scurried down the stairs. I stuffed everything under my chest.

We spent the next forty-eight hours in my room reading through everything. Nowhere was there a record of the wife's death. We did find a map of the grounds, the cotton fields, the slaves' quarters. All of it meticulously hand drawn. There was a record of a fire that correlated to the day before the owner died and five slaves listed as dead.

Only a skeleton staff remained so into the night I searched. I had to know, maybe because I knew my history and humble beginnings were birthed from slavery or maybe I was inadvertently searching for a clue to my own past. Either way I stayed up and was glad I did.

Excitement shot through me like a bullet! I found it. A birth, approximately eight months after the death of the husband and the last one recorded in any ledger. A boy named Isaac Hartley, five pounds, three ounces, and seventeen inches long. They gave all the slaves their last name, so each was a Hartley like the owners. I wondered if they kept that name.

It dawned on me as I considered waking Johnie, who snored quietly on Robin's bed, that someone cared enough about these people, these slaves, to record everything. Even then, even though it was a way of life they knew, they knew colored people were far more than livestock but humans with souls and hearts and love. They just couldn't admit it and let their empire tumble.

I had a name. Isaac Hartley. I dreamed of a child, umber skin and strong facial features.

Marva

After a breakfast of cereal and milk, Johnie and I rushed outside ready to venture the grounds. We had the map; of course, it looked different today. The cotton fields no longer existed, filled in by wildflowers and trees but the river that was really Hartley Creek, on the map anyways, hadn't changed.

We counted the paces from the house to the edge of the property and followed it. Headstones rose from the ground surrounded by a low stone wall. I gazed on, my mind filled with ideas, pausing for a beat. Johnie looked over her shoulder.

"No," she said, shaking her head. "Nope. I don't do graveyards even in daylight."

I twisted my mouth in thought. Ella Louise could be buried here, right here under my nose, but by Johnie's firm expression I knew to keep walking and explore it on my own. Maybe Robin or Lissa would join me. They'd be excited when I told them everything.

I hurried forward, catching up with Johnie who reached the stream. The sun moved with us as we walked along the water's edge. Tall, leafy trees providing shade. The spot where Greta claimed the slave's quarters were was all wrong. That area had been cotton fields. An assortment of color burst from the ground as wildflowers bloomed. The teapot tree marked the spot as it watched over the land.

We stopped for lunch, Cook -- that's what everyone called her – was nice enough to pack us sandwiches, fruit, and juice for our adventure. The grass filled in, we sat in the same spot, or close enough as we had initiation night, and ate. Parulas sang a melody from the treetops and butterflies flitted from flower to flower.

White pillowy clouds dotted the sky as they moved over the sun. Counting our paces, we skipped to the opposite edge of the property from where we started in search of the slaves quarters. The place becoming more familiar with each skip.

I lay the map down as we both stared at the little cabin. It's all that was left. According to the map a great complex of several little homes built in rows once sat next to it.

I tried to imagine what it looked like. Thirty-one little homes in two parallel rows. The middle an area for congregating. "Come on." I bounded past the little cabin.

Johnie stared apprehensively. Her face pinched into a knot. "Maybe we shouldn't."

"Do you *see* something?"

"Not anything new," she responded, unpinching her face.

"It's OK, really. See." I took a step backwards.

She rocked on her feet then took one small step. "OK."

No sign of foundations or fire pits or anything was there. Wildflowers had grown over everything that ever was, erasing the existence of people. It was a little disappointing. I hoped to at least find a cement block or remnants of a framed foundation. It was all removed. Sorrow tugged at my heart as if these people weren't worth missing even though a direct contradiction to the meticulous records.

Seeing my excitement plummet, my lips sink, Johnie said, "I get it. You feel a connection. That baby was mixed like you but what you're searching for can't be found here."

I mulled those words in my head. She was right. It was the connectedness, but my link was at White Oak. Not as grand as Ella Louise, it was still a very large and fine plantation for its time. I hadn't explored with the same eyes I used now. Drawn to the child who was forbidden like me, lost his parents like me, I was seeking answers.

It was that moment I knew this summer I had to search White Oak with the same eye with which I searched Ella Louise now. That's where I'd find my answers. The spooky, hidden room in the attic was a place to start but I didn't think I had the guts to return to it. For a time it gave me a reason to return to a place that harbored so many abusive and neglectful memories.

"What are you girls doing out here?"

I jumped at the sound of the voice, landing turned around. A light-colored woman, similar to my color stood outside the back of the cabin, hands on her hips, staring at us.

I was speechless. It was Johnie who spoke up, "We... um... we go to the school."

She walked towards us. "Uh huh. I see and you had nothing better to do than explore my land?"

Johnie and I glanced at each other. "We thought it belonged to the school," I offered in explanation.

"Well, come on," she said waving us towards her and a wooden table and chairs on the back side of the cabin.

She pulled out a chair and sat. We joined her alright, hands in our laps as we dropped into the seats across from her.

Resting her hands on the weathered wood table, she smiled. Wrinkles ebbed from the corners of her eyes. Silver streaks stood out against the blackness of her hair that was neatly tied back in a ponytail. "It used to belong to the plantation but when the school bought it my family was given this land here."

"Why?" I asked. As the unfiltered word slipped from my mouth, I knew I shouldn't have said it.

It didn't faze her, nor did she correct it. "Because my family sharecropped this land, kept up the cotton fields even after the owners passed. When the school bought it, they gave my family a chunk and you're looking at it."

My eyes widened into saucers and I rested my hands on the table. "Your family was here. What about the baby?"

"Sugar, lots of babies were born here. Which one are you referrin' to?"

Maybe I was pushing the envelope too far but I wanted so badly to know. "Well, Ella Louise and the slave's baby."

She curled her hands over mine. "Plantation owners had their way with slaves in many ways. Every plantation had mixed babies running around. Ella Louise wasn't any different."

"What do you mean?" Johnie asked, eyebrows arched.

"I mean the owner was my great, great, great, great granddaddy."

I allowed that thought to process for several seconds before, "Damen," slipped quietly out of my mouth.

She nodded.

All those meticulous records, all those slaves born, how many belonged to the owner himself?

The lady interrupted my thoughts, completely changing the subject. "You're here because you're curious but I've been waiting for you...Both of you are *touched* with a certain sight." Her dark eyes grew serious as she leaned in. "Initiation is a time when girls with the *touch* see things. Alone out here in the night with the haunts the past meshes with the present.

You see, someone who is as talented as you sustained childhood trauma. The brain rewires itself to bury the trauma. You must get past that to gain control."

She curled her hand around Johnie's, still holding onto mine. She glanced at me first, searching my eyes, digging into my buried past. "There's a lot of darkness in you; abuse, sadness, confusion, neglect. You have barriers that run more than the thickness of your skull so you'll have to really dig to find the incident that started it all."

She turned to Johnie as I considered her words and how true each one was. "Yours is on the top, waiting to come forward."

"The night we... uh... of the initiation, we saw something. Both of us heard something. A girl from the school is missing," I finally blurted.

The woman sighed. "You shared a vision, but you say a girl is missing?"

We nodded simultaneously.

Her eyebrows knitted. "You think it happened here?"

I swallowed as my throat suddenly became parched and nodded.

She leaned back in her chair, stared into the sky and folded her arms over her chest. "What exactly did you see?"

I fed her my story and Johnie hers. She clung to each word that escaped our mouths.

She dropped her eyes from the sky and met our eyes. "The two of you are connected. Before you can solve any crimes, if any have occurred, you need to gain control of your vision. Sort through it."

We stared at her expectantly.

Her dark, soft eyes searched ours then she walked to the back door. "Come inside. I need to show you something." Noting we glanced at each other she opened the door and waved us in.

We stood, I took in a deep breath, and Johnie reached for my hand. Sweat moistened our grip as we marched inside.

She struck a match and lit a candle on a narrow table by the futon then pulled the drapes. Pointing to Johnie she said, "Lay down." She gave her a moment to sit on the futon and lie back while kneeling onto the wood floor. "Close your eyes, breathe in the aromas. Let them percolate in your mind. I'm taking your hand now. Breathe in, breathe out. Follow my voice."

She waved me closer and pointed to the spot on the floor beside her. I sat without hesitation. "It's dark and the fog is thick and heavy. Focus your mind. What do you see?"

Johnie's breathing slowed as if in a trance. "I see a fire from the window of the cabin. Its flames look promising. I want to run inside but I can't. Debbie is staring through the window and a man, tall with wide shoulders, appears behind her. He has a ski mask on his head." Her body shudders visibly for a second.

"Shh... what else do you see?" the lady asks, her voice as calming as the candle.

Johnie's neck twitches. "In his hand is a gun. The moonlight shines on the barrel. Debbie turns around and then... a scream fills my ears and I hurl the rock in my hand. It hits the man in the head and he... he..." Her breathing becomes rapid, her eyes move beneath their lids then pop open and she sits up gasping for breath.

The woman wrapped her arms around Johnie and rubbed her head.

When Johnie got her breath and voice back she asked, 'What happened?"

"You are on the precipice of remembering something big." The woman stood and helped Johnie off the futon. "The sun is setting. You need to get back to the school." She walked us toward the door. "Before you go I want the two of you to do what we did today. Hold each other's hands, comfort one another and oh!" She rushed to one of the cabinets and swung it open.

She turned around and in her hand was a candle. "This is special. I make them myself. It's infused with lemon balm, lavender, cloves, rosemary, and a pinch of black pepper. Always burn this. It will help. Do this exercise as many times a week as you can." She wrapped it in tissue. "I'm Marva. Now shoo, both of you."

Nearly pushing us out the door we didn't skip or walk back, we ran full speed, but I'd swear we heard her call after us, 'I'm here on Thursdays.'

Hartley Legacy

We returned in time for dinner. Neither of us ate much as our minds were a frenzy.

Even with the flutter that someone, a grown-up, was touched like us, understood it, had control and wanted to teach us, I hadn't forgotten about the baby -- Isaac Hartley. We sat in comfortable computer chairs that rolled and spinned as Johnie went to the county's website and searched its records.

Online records didn't date back more than fifty years. "We'll have to go in person," Johnie said after her arduous search.

"What about his name?" I asked.

She typed it in the search bar and a list of Isaac Hartleys came up, most living now. A brain blast hit her and with hopeful eyes she said, "I got it! There is a website that has family records. My mom used it to trace our ancestry. We can try that."

Her fingers pounded the keys with precision as she searched for Isaac Hartley. I spun in the chair. Computers weren't my thing. I was only beginning to understand them. It was the one study I had problems with and didn't have an A.

She pointed to the screen. "Look."

She found Hartleys in Louisiana dating back to pre-civil war. It was a lead. She clicked on names and profiles, found them on social media and I scribbled anything worthy of panning out.

"Time for bed girls," Ms. Timble said, standing in the tear-drop doorway, her peppered hair pulled back into a bun.

Neither of us able to sleep, we sneaked back to the library, making sure first that Ms. Timble was in her quarters. Through the night, Johnie typed and clicked, tracing Hartleys in Lousianna. I dozed in and out of sleep in the spinning chair.

"I got it," she said, enthusiasm lighting her face. "There was never an Isaac Hartley but there was an Isaac Hart, parents are listed as Ben and Cecelia Hart. He was born about the time we know baby Isaac was, even better there's a living relative in New Orleans who owns a voodoo shop in the French Quarter."

"We have to go!"

"I got that covered too. I heard the girls talking. At the end of the year we get a field trip to the Louisiana State Museum located in the French Quarter." She folded her arms across her chest in satisfaction.

I liked how our minds were connected.

In the morning I woke with a thought that burned into my brain. Ben and Cecelia sounded so familiar. I searched through a couple ledgers until I found them. Baby Isaac didn't have parents listed but a Ben and Cecelia lived on the plantation at the time of his birth. I was another step closer.

A blanket of thick black clouds hung in the sky from the time we stepped onto the bus. I should have taken it as a warning.

New Orleans was so large. I'd never seen so many buildings stacked like cubes one right to the other. Each structure carried a personality of its own. Various colors, balcony sizes, and storefronts. Neon lights shone steady, brightening the gloomy day. My eyes were a wonder as they soaked in the surrounding magic.

Johnie and I fell behind, ready to make our break. She had the address and mapped it. My heart pitter-pattered in my chest with the prospect of meeting a relative of Isaac Hart.

Lissa glanced over her shoulder and smiled at me then whispered into Robin's ear. They slowed and waited for us to catch up. "What are you planning?" Lissa asked.

"Nothing." I bit my lip to keep from saying more.

"I know you better. We've heard you talking and we want in." Her eyes fixed on Johnie and me instead of the grand structure we stood in front of with its long facade and round porticos that spanned the front of the building.

Johnie rocked on her heels and Lissa and Robin gave us each a stern eye. She swallowed. "We found a relative we think is the baby from the initiation story and she has a store only a couple blocks from here."

I cringed at her words and pulled my hands behind my back as we shuffled through the entrance. All of us keeping our voices off as Ms. Timble and our history teacher counted our heads. Once the tour guide met us we spoke low.

"You know that's just a story Greta tells to scare everyone," Robin offered.

I'd told them about finding the ledgers and even showed them, pointing out various names and dates but I hadn't told them about Johnie's research. It was true we hadn't found a death certificate for the wife but we had proof of the baby. Which gave me an idea. "You can help. We'll go visit Destiny Hart while the two of you go to the office of vital records to search for the wife's death certificate."

Lissa considered the offer carefully as her mouth twisted into a knot. "OK, where is it?"

This way we'd get done twice as fast and meet back at the museum. If one group arrived before the other we'd cover for the others. It was a deal, sealed with a high five.

The group carried on as we took quiet steps backwards until they were out of sight. Johnie and I headed for the voodoo shop while Robin and Lissa headed the other direction. A coating of drizzle covered our clothes and hair by the time we reached the voodoo shop.

It was quaint which wasn't the word I was expecting to use. Purple shutters nailed to the wall and crown molding outside under the awning gave it an inviting and timeless presence. Inside, candles, dolls, strange masks, skulls - lots of skulls -- bright furniture, drums, and jewelry hung on the walls and were stuffed into each corner. I didn't think they could stuff one more item into the store.

The store was shaped like a rectangle and all the way in the back was a wooden counter with a register. Behind it were long strings of wood beads leading into a back room. I'd replayed in my head what I would say. Johnie and I had practiced it but at that moment my mind went blank. I think Johnie's did too as we stepped in front of the register.

My palms sweaty and my heart pounding like someone beating on one of the drums. I thought it might jump right out of my chest. I gathered spit to moisturize my suddenly dry mouth. A tall, thin guy no more than sixteen with olive skin and chiseled features stood behind the register. A black T-shirt stenciled Destiny's Home of Voodoo in white creepy lettering like the sign that hung out front.

I swallowed the small wad of spit I gathered and stepped closer to the register.

"Can I help you?" asked the man. His voice deep and low, almost scary.

We both nodded but I spoke, "Is Destiny here?"

His lips curled into a crooked smile and dimples creased each cheek. "She's busy with a customer, maybe I can help?" He leaned his elbows on the counter and leaned over them.

"No, we need to see her," I said.

"Umm... OK. Well you shop around and when she's finished, I'll call you back."

Shopping or looking at anything in that store gave me the creeps. Wooden masks with vacant eyes and colorful feathers watched us. The wait seemed like it went on forever. A lady in a high-collared purple dress and a fancy upswing hairstyle walked through the wooden beads. The heels of her knee-high boots clicking against the wooden floor.

"Are you ready?" the guy asked, freaking me out so badly I jumped.

We nodded and he led us behind the wooden beads. Johnie and I stayed close. I know she was every bit as scared as me. Light danced on the walls from the many large three wick candles spread around the room. An old, old lady, her ashy skin thin and wrinkled as papier-mâché sat at a table. Candlelight giving it an unnatural glow. A deep red scarf over her head, covering any hair she had left. I placed Destiny's age as at least one hundred but maybe I was overestimating.

She pointed with a distended skinny finger towards two chairs opposite her. I glanced over my shoulder at the guy. He shrugged in response and his facial expression said, *I warned you.*

"What can I possibly help you with today?" Destiny said.

Johnie and I shared glances then I cleared my nervous throat. "We thought you might be able to help us... um... with something. A relative of yours, we think."

She leaned her head back and her voice cracked with age. "Oh, I see, and who would that be?"

Sweat beaded on my forehead as I spoke. "Isaac Hart. He was your ancestor."

Her face so wrinkled it was hard to tell, but I'm pretty sure more wrinkles deepened beneath her hairline. "And what is it you want to know about Isaac?"

"Well, um... was he... the son of Ella Louise Hartley?" I spit it out and no matter what she said at least I gave it a try.

"Why would you think that? Those Hartleys were bad business. You from that school?"

We both nodded.

"You listen to me. That man didn't die of any voodoo curse. He was killed, murdered probably by that wife of his. All her beauty she was as rotten as he was, every bit."

"You… you are related?" Johnie stuttered.

She stood, latched her hand onto a gold cane with a skull handle and shuffled towards a shelf. Pulling something off, she shuffled back and sat, resting her cane against the table. "I'm a Hart by marriage. My late husband was Isaac's grandson."

At that statement I wondered if she was a hundred, maybe even more.

She laid a picture on the table. It was old and yellowed, of a family. The edges withered and worn. She pointed to a man and my eyes followed her finger, dark curls covered his head and his skin color was hard to tell in the picture but wasn't quite white nor quite black. Almost chameleon, like my own. "That's Isaac."

My jaw dropped in awe. "He's so…"

"White," she finished my words. "Like us." She pointed to me then herself. "The Hartleys were a family if you know what I mean but his parents were Ben and Cecelia." Her profound words sent my mind aflutter. *What was she saying?*

Her dark eyes set inside a web of wrinkles stared into mine and she restated maybe she'd forgot but her mind seemed sharp as a tack. "Damen wasn't murdered by no voodoo. Someone killed him and I'm betting it was that wife. Always running around on her with the slaves. Not like they had a choice when the master called, *they* did even if they didn't want to. Right under her nose. Wasn't but a matter a time the goose would think it OK to do as the gander."

I wasn't quite sure what all that meant but assumed it meant she wasn't the only person in the marriage that had black babies -- so did Mr. Hartley, and lots of them.

Her eyes narrowed and she clucked her tongue. "You seem like smart girls so I'm going to tell you this. Be careful how deep you dig into this well. You may not find what you're looking for at the bottom." Her words mirroring Marva's.

The beaded curtains drew back, making a scratching sound, and Johnie and I nearly jumped out of our chairs.

The guy stood in the doorway, so tall his head almost touched the top. "Gram, Mrs. Bickson is here."

She nodded, confirming she understood, then looked deep and square into my eyes. "If there's anything else you need my great grandson, Cole, will help you out."

We rose from our chairs. "Thank you," I offered. It wasn't polite not to use my manners even though I wanted to run straight back to the museum.

We scurried out of the room of horrors, running smack into the guy I guessed was Cole. "I'm sorry," I apologized as I stepped back from his chest. I didn't even notice the woman who walked right past us.

He leaned back against the counter. "It's really beginning to come down out there hard. You may want to wait a bit."

He seemed friendly enough with his infectious smile and dimples. One day I'd be forced to see Malery again and that stupid doll, so considered wasting a few extra minutes in the store may be worth my while. "What can you tell me about voodoo dolls?"

His upper lip curled. "Well that depends on whether the person using it actually knows what they're doing. Most people think of them as something used to curse someone but there're far easier ways to do that."

I walked around the counter, Johnie staying close. "So they don't really work?"

"They can, but are usually used for healing and love. Most of what you see on TV and stuff is commercialized. We sell that stuff here too. People want to bring home an authentic voodoo item when they visit New Orleans, but real voodoo isn't like that. Is someone threatening or bullying you?" His brows creased with concern.

"It's silly, just my cousin, but I never felt anything when he pricked it or choked it." I didn't mention the visions it sent me into. There might be some kind of magic in it, just not the kind Malery thought.

"I tell you what, it doesn't really work unless the person believes. Next time he tries it I want you to spit, not directly on him or even on something he values, and say what you want to happen like," his face became serious, "may your tongue wrap into a knot when you speak of me."

I chuckled. "Really?"

He shrugged. "Sure, if he believes it. You don't even have to spit but it adds spice to the curse." He grabbed a business card off the counter and flipped it over, scribbled something and handed it to me. "He gives you a hard time and you need something stronger than a simple curse, call me."

A phone number with the name Cole across the top was on the card. I slipped it into my pocket. "Thank you."

Greta Deserves It

On the bus ride home, we sat in the back and shared our stories. Robin and Lissa came up empty-handed. There was no death certificate or record for one Ella Louise Hartley in New Orleans or Louisiana. Which meant at least that part of the story wasn't true.

After dinner and curfew. We waited for the ladies to check rooms then Johnie snuck over, we lit the candle and worked on our memories the way Marva taught us. Robin and Lissa were quite used to it by now but were usually asleep when we did it.

Johnie held my hand as I recalled the events of initiation night. The fireplace, the window, the man with his cloudy blue eyes, even the blood-drenched knife in his hand was the same, but the foggy night changed to four concrete walls with a rounded ceiling. Beams stretched over the ceiling with pictures between them but it was too dark to tell what they were.

Marble tiles covered the walls. The man was gone and I was alone in the structure. Clunk... clunk... and the pitter patter of feet made me jump. The urge to run seizing every inch of my body but when I tried my foot slipped and I came crashing down.

My eyes popped open and I stared into Johnie's face. "I know where Sam is!"

I was too anxious to eat breakfast, my stomach doubling over in knots. There was only one place on the grounds we hadn't been and there was no plausible explanation why Sam might have visited there that morning unless she went to find us and, the spot vacant, she had begun her own search.

We told Robin and Lissa about my vision and they insisted on joining us as we dashed towards the stone wall. I reached it first and halted as I stared at the many weathered headstones and, in the back corner surrounded by trees, a mausoleum.

I stepped over the wall and walked among the headstones, followed by Lissa, Robin, and Johnie, who paused as I walked up the two cement steps of the mausoleum. It was a simple, rectangular structure, engraved with fanciful designs over the door. I bit my lip nervously then pressed my hand against it, pushing any fear into a small place inside me like I did the day I crawled through the vents at White Oak.

It wasn't locked or as heavy as it seemed and opened right up. I didn't even have to walk inside to smell the putrid odor of death. Choking and gagging, I leaned my head over, my breakfast spilling onto the concrete alcove. After a minute I caught my breath and pulled my shirt over my nose. Sam lay stretched over a bench sitting square in the middle of the room. Dried blood covering her pant legs and puddled on the floor beneath her. A stream elongating towards the door where the concrete floor wasn't as even as it appeared.

Under her body was the murder weapon. The cement bench had matching decorative posts no more than two inches high between the arm and back rest. She'd fallen onto one, in her own fear, impaling herself. It wasn't the scene that made tears drain from my eyes but that she was alone.

She'd died for no reason except Greta. It was her fault. I'd disliked her, but that day I'd say I truly hated her.

The sun's warmth soaked through my skin. My eyes closed and hand on the locket around my neck, I tried to envision my mom the way I did at White Oak under the cypress tree. I imagined the leaves swaying in a gentle breeze carrying the hanging moss with them. It was the solace I needed to get my thoughts together. They were interrupted when I heard muffled voices and crying.

Listening, I followed the sound. Three girls I recognized as former Scraps had someone pinned against a tree. "You're an evil bitch!" one of them said.

Another took a swing and landed with a thud.

"She was my friend," came out in sobs.

I moved closer, hiding myself behind a tree. My eyes wide. Greta was pinned against a tree with what looked like a rope around her chest.

"You think anyone believes that after what you did to us? Humiliating us, tormenting us for years. My journal, my private thoughts, spread throughout the school. Do you know what that feels like?" the tall one with long dark hair in a

French braid seethed as she got right up in Greta's face then spit.

"And my bloody underwear hanging from the flagpole. I was twelve and just started my period," another with short blond hair and a toothpick body said, throwing dirt in Greta's face. "That's what I think of you."

Tears streamed through the dirt, mingling with the spit, and trailed her lovely porcelain cheeks. As much as I hated her it wasn't right what they were doing.

"We'll be back in the morning at first light so you can experience a night out here alone with the ghosts and wild animals," said the one with the braid.

Greta screamed, choking back sobs. "You can't do this. We go home tomorrow. Please. I didn't do it! It was an accident."

The girls ran off, chuckling. The tree trunk wide, I scooted back as they scampered past me. Once they were out of sight, I scurried towards Greta whose head was hung over her chest, sobbing.

"Greta."

She lifted her head. Dirt filled the corners of her round, blue eyes. Underneath it all she was still very beautiful, like a China doll that got dropped in the mud. "What? Are you here to finish what they started?"

I shook my head. "No. I heard some of it."

She sniffled. "Well then what are we waiting for, untie me!" she ordered.

I stepped back, even tied to a tree, spit, mud, and tears mottling her delicate face, she still wasn't humbled.

Noting my backwards motion, she begged, "Please, I'm sorry. I... I... can you please untie me? I've never done any harm to you."

"But you have others, and Sam too. I know those girls hated Sam. Anyone of them could have pushed her into the poster on that bench but they didn't. It was a horrible, horrible accident."

Water gushed from her eyes and her face scrunched into a beautiful mess as she wailed, incoherent words choked with sobs coming from her mouth.

I went to her. "Promise me there'll be no more initiation, no more Scraps, no more bullying others. Promise me."

Her wail slowed to choked sobs. "I promise."

"Pinky swear it." I held out my pinky to her.

She lifted a pinky, her arms tied with the rope around her chest. "I can't lift my hand."

I lowered my hand, my pinky meeting hers. "Say it now. No more cruelty to others."

She repeated my words through her sniffles. I went around the tree and started untying the knots. It took a minute as they were tight but once I got it the rope fell to her ankles. She did the most unexpected thing and wrapped her arms around me, lowering her head to my shoulder. "Thank you," she whispered. I pulled my arms around her in a tight hug and it felt good.

It was that moment that marked something I didn't fully understand yet. She lifted her head off my shoulder and stared into my eyes then tilted her head and brought her lips to mine. She pressed them against mine then pushed her tongue into my mouth through my parted lips.

The experience took me by surprise but I didn't stop her. On the contrary, I worked my tongue with hers. The action was natural and that moment seemed to go on even though it wasn't more than a minute or so. She drew back. "I'm sorry." She stepped backwards and lowered her eyes as if she'd done something wrong. "I know I'm not supposed to like girls like that and I don't in that way, except you. It's all I've thought about since you got here."

I didn't know what to say. Frozen in place and my tongue lost, I stared at her.

She glanced at me hopefully and seeing something on my face that displeased her she backed away more. "I'm sorry. Thank you," she said and turned on her heel.

"Wait," I called. "I'm surprised that's all. I've never kissed anyone like that, but I liked it. I want to do it again." Those words spilled from my mouth before I even had a chance to think about them. Feelings, desire, bubbled inside of me with excitement. I wanted to spend the rest of the day kissing her.

Her dirty lips spread into a smile and she grabbed my hand. I was reminded of the day she wouldn't touch me, pulled away as if I was a leper, now it didn't seem to bother her, in fact, she wanted it.

Our arms swung hand in hand as we strolled through the trees to the stream. Finding a fallen log, we sat on it. She traced my face with a finger, then my mouth. "You have beautiful lips," she said, her fingers fondling my mouth.

My eyes drifted to her blossoming chest. The tips of her breasts showing above the cut of her T-shirt. Hesitantly I brought my hand to them. Meeting her gaze, I traced their soft edges. Her skin was like silk. Her lips pressed against mine again. Urges in my nether regions pushed into my lips as our tongues swirled inside each other's mouths. My fingers gently circling her breasts.

She traced a wandering finger down my chest and abdomen, pausing as she reached the waistband of my loose shorts. Excitement filled me up and I wanted to force her hands down my pants to quell the desire stirring down there.

The crunching of leaves stopped us immediately. We both heard it, our eyes searching from where it came when,across the river, I spotted something moving. "There." I pointed.

"I see it," she said as she called, "Come on out. What are you? Shy? Never saw two girls kissing?"

The bushes moved and a head and torso rose from behind them. Standing across the river no more than fifteen feet was a boy, tall, gangly, with short, dirty blond hair. The rim of his swim trunks showed above the top of the shrubbery. It was hard to tell but I was sure he was blushing as his cheeks looked especially rosy.

"I just come down here for a swim. I didn't mean to interrupt you." His eyes darted to the log we sat on. I supposed he was embarrassed as me.

Greta wasn't bothered and, if she was, she didn't show it. "I think you were enjoying what you saw."

His eyes still focused on the log or maybe the ground, he stuttered, "I... um."

"Just admit it. I bet you got a boner watching us. That's why you're hiding in those bushes. Come on out. Let's see," she jeered.

Backed into a corner she came out fighting. That's what made her mean as a rattlesnake. I jabbed her. "Don't taunt him. You pinky swore."

"You're right," she admitted. "But I really want to see it."

I furrowed my brows in confusion.

"His boner, you know, his erect penis. I want to know what it looks like. I'm curious," she insisted, her voice filled with innocence and teenage wonder.

Filled with curiosity and arousal, I wanted to see it too. Urges pulsed through me with a vengeance, but I knew better.

I stood to take my leave and she pulled my arm. "Don't leave," she begged, and so I stayed and we left, talking the whole way. She explained how she had an older stepbrother and caught him once 'spanking the monkey,' she called it. It was before she was old enough for private school. She was only seven or eight and her mom asked her to get him for dinner. When she opened the door his hand was lying in his bed, his other hand caressing his penis. He was moaning and so focused on what he was doing he didn't notice her in the doorway.

She watched in awe, unable to move or speak. He finally growled and creamy stuff erupted from the tip of his penis. That's when she got her footing back and ran from the room.

"What happened next?" I asked.

"I only recently remembered this and you can't ever tell anyone. Swear it on your mother's grave." Her face somber.

"I swear on my mother's grave."

She explained how he started coming into her room at night. He'd cover her mouth and threaten to kill her mom if she ever said a word to anyone, then touched her private areas and did other horrible, sexual things to her. All she wanted was for something really bad to happen to him so he'd leave her alone.

Her behavior and hatefulness of the world began to make a lot of sense as I remembered Malery's cruelness towards me. He didn't do those things to me but abused me in many other ways. My aunt too and, when I thought about it, I didn't like my uncle because of his wandering eye. Always watching me from the corner of it. When he crawled into my bed wasn't by mistake. He was drunk, but knew what he was doing. The hard object pressed between my legs, his hands fondling my small developing nubs.

She stopped walking. "You know that day at the cabin? I knew you and Johnie didn't hurt Sam. I saw it, but I hoped to see more, thinking maybe you knew something but you are so filled with darkness it scared me to touch you. It also aroused me. I saw things, horrible things."

What exactly was she telling me?

She sat cross-legged on the ground and motioned for me to join her. I did, my brain sifting through her words. She continued talking as she twirled the grass with her finger. "Initiation was always about finding girls like us --

broken, touched. The night of mine, I found Marva. She took me in and helped me break through and remembered the awful things my stepbrother did to me. Over time I've gained control and when I touch people I see the awful things they've been through. No one, though, ever moved me like you." She continued to twirl the grass. "When those girls graduated. They too were touched. Alone in the woods here brings out the scary."

"This school is for broken people?"

"No." She chuckled. "But some are. Girls who go to boarding school fit into three categories; ones whose parents don't have time for them but have money to send them away, ones whose parents don't have money but want the prestige of a fine education and acceptance to the best colleges and last, ones who are broken. Their parents send them off because they're scared and don't know what else to do. We fit into the last category." She glanced up at me, her pools of blue solemn and lonely.

In the Crypt

I woke up that night after a dream I lost as soon as my eyes fluttered open. My only thought Ella Louise Hartley. Greta may have triggered something, opening up the way she did. Either way I had something to do, something that nibbled at the back of my mind since finding Sam.

I slipped out of bed and quietly headed downstairs, stopping in the kitchen and grabbing a flashlight. I sprinted as fast as my two feet could carry me back to the mausoleum. I kept my mind focused so I wouldn't see the shadows moving in the trees and cautiously walked up the steps. Crime scene tape covered the doorway, so I pushed above it. The door opened, hazy moonlight streaming through the window. That night was foggy and the moon's light wasn't visible. She wouldn't have seen much.

I took a deep breath and shone my flashlight against the marble plates of the crypts as I pulled the crime scene tape up and walked beneath it. Noises and scratches sounded behind me. I didn't turn around as I didn't want to end up like Sam. She'd let it get to her. I wasn't doing that. The sounds were probably just branches scraping the roof, I told myself as I shone the flashlight on each plate until I came to the one I was searching for.

Ella Louise Hartley 1833 -1859. The scratching grew louder as I stepped towards the crypt. It was like she was scratching to get free. "It's your imagination," I whispered to the air. I placed the flashlight between my legs, shining the beam upwards as I took one last, long breath and let it out. A drummer marching in my chest. I pulled the drawer out slowly.

I didn't look until the drawer was out a few inches. When I did look, I expected to see a coffin, not what I saw. It was empty, nothing. That explained the absence of a death certificate but it didn't tell me what really happened to her.

A loud clank and more scratching made me jump and I fell backwards. My head hitting the edge of the bench. A sharp pain radiated through my neck and spinal cord. The flashlight fell and I swore I saw the edges of a dress move across the floor. Scrambling to my hands and knees, I crawled to the door. I wasn't going to stand and fall against the bench the way Sam did. When I reached the taped doorway, I realized I'd dropped my flashlight.

I had no choice but to go back. It was dark and the moon's light wasn't enough. My breaths short as fear rode me. Its nails clung to my back as I crawled backwards and reached for the flashlight, without looking. My eyes focused on the floor beneath my face.

I grabbed the solid, rounded object when I felt its cold, metal edges against my hand. Something soft brushed over my arm and I pulled it back, flashlight clenched tight in my fist as I crawled back to the door and slipped under the tape. I never glanced back as I ran like lightning to the school, flung the wide tear-drop door open and finally stopped when I dropped onto my bed, pulling the covers over my head.

Summer

ur eyes filled with tears that streamed across our cheeks. Johnie and I hugged and said goodbye. A forever goodbye as her mom and new stepdad weren't sending her back in the fall. They told her it wasn't safe because a girl got killed and I think what made it worse was she was there when the body was found.

Her parents, with their stern faces, pulled her away from me but not before she slipped a paper into my hand. I watched until the car was out of sight then unfolded the paper.

I love you, Debbie. Stay in touch

Her phone number was on the bottom of the paper. I folded it back and stuffed it into the zipper section of my small suitcase.

Already uneasy about going back to White Oak, Malery, and the tension between my grandma and my aunt, I sat on the large suitcase, balancing it with my feet. Greta strolled past me, talking with a beautiful, porcelain-faced woman with thick blond hair styled perfectly around her face. A flowered summer dress and light, see-through jacket over her shoulders. I guessed Greta's mom as they looked so much alike.

A man, with thick glasses and dark hair, lifted her suitcases into the trunk of an impressive convertible car. He placed an arm around Greta's mom then opened the door for both Greta and her mom. I figured that was her stepdad. She never said what happened to her stepbrother or if her mom ever found out what was happening. Greta unrolled the window and gave me a wink as the car pulled out.

Lissa and Robin both left early but not without our goodbyes. I shifted restlessly on the suitcase, one of the few girls left when a long car pulled up with a sign for me. The drive was long and arduous. My trepidation reaching maximum overload when the car pulled into the long driveway. My grandmother waiting on the porch.

That evening turned out to be not so bad, as Miss. Dresdan made me a large meal and cake. We talked and I told them about my friends, leaving out the stuff they didn't need to know. My grandma didn't say it, but I was sure she knew about me finding Sam's body.

After dinner and a shower, I slipped into bed when my grandmother entered my room and sat on the edge of my bed. "I'm sorry for sending you away. For making you stay in the attic that horrible day." The sadness in her eyes overwhelming. Wrinkles webbed her once-stunning face.

Did she know I sneaked into a secret room and down the stairs? No, it was an apt apology and heartfelt but didn't take away the betrayal. "Where's Aunt?"

Her face dropped more if that was possible. "I sent her on a cruise. Losing your Uncle was too much. I thought it would be good for her." That was her way of saying she won't be here this summer. I took care of it.

"What about Malery?"

"He's working and taking classes. He won't be home until Christmas, probably."

I sensed Malery didn't want to be here. I think it was the only thing we really had in common besides our family. "It's OK, you know."

"What?"

I played with the edges of my crimson comforter. "Sending me to the school. I like it and I have friends. I want to go back. But the attic... that wasn't OK and never will be."

She nodded. "I am sorry. I panicked and wanted to protect you."

"Protect me from what?" I spat.

"Nothing, I panicked. Get some rest."

I placed my hand on hers. "What happened between you, my mom and Aunt Olivia? Don't lie to me either, I'm a big girl."

She leaned back onto my headboard and squeezed my hand. "Yes, you are. Well, I guess it's time you knew. It started the year your mom entered Ella Louise as a seventh grader, like you. Olivia was a senior and I guess during the year tensions grew between them. Both were beautiful girls but your mom had a little extra something that made her shine inside and out, much like you."

She tilted her head as if searching for flaws in the paint. "She had the most amazing, eye-catching coloring. Her skin was like a chameleon. In a group of white folks she looked white as them. In a group of black folks she was every bit as dark as them. People noticed her and she became very popular. She loved her older sister, admired her more than anyone. Olivia, though, was always more reserved and jealous of the doting and attention your Alma received. Well, that summer when they returned home the rubber band between them snapped...

"Olivia met her first boyfriend but, after being introduced to Alma, he came over more and more even when Olivia wasn't home. Always bringing little things for Alma. I thought it was an innocent young man trying to make good with his girlfriend's sister. It was anything but innocent. At thirteen she was intimidated, flattered, and scared. When he kissed her, she ran to Olivia and told her, thinking she was doing the sisterly thing. Olivia blew up at her, locked herself away in her room and cried for days. She loved the young man, thought they'd be married, but after that she never saw him again. Alma was crushed and wished she'd kept her mouth shut. She hated seeing her so upset." Grandma paused for a second before continuing. Her weary eyes searched mine.

Olivia went off to college and, upon graduation, was engaged to marry Uncle Lawrence. They had the wedding at White Oak. She was brimming with glee. After those few years Olivia forgave Alma and made her Maid of Honor at the wedding. It was after they came back from their honeymoon that old demons resurfaced when she caught him coming from my mom's room one night. She accused them both of cheating. She wouldn't listen to either of them. Grandma couldn't tell the truth from the lies, thinking the worst, and my mom covering so her sister that she so admired wouldn't hate her again.

Olivia turned him out, turned him away until she learned she was pregnant. He told her what she wanted to hear, whether truth or lies, and begged for her forgiveness. She gave it and Malery was born several months later. Even though she claimed to forgive him she didn't, and stopped having marital relations with him.

It made Alma more and more desirable. Young and attractive, and Lawrence sex-deprived, he made passes at her in private. Tried and tried to get his way with her but she'd push him away over and over just like his wife. One summer afternoon he followed Alma through the woods and had his way with her. Alma's boyfriend, the man she was sneaking off to see, heard her screaming and came to her rescue, pulling Lawrence off her. He brought her back to the house, her dress ripped and hanging off her shoulders, dirt and grass in her hair.

She went to her room and packed a bag, left White Oak and never returned. Uncle Lawrence claimed he didn't do anything, that he tried to help her. That the man who brought her to the house was guilty. Grandma knew it was a lie. She'd seen how he looked at her, studied her curves. But, with a baby, Olivia chose to believe him and forever disavowed Alma, calling her slut, a cheap trick.

I remembered my mother's letters. The man who saved her that day was my father and my brothers' father. She loved him very much, yet kept him secret. Knowing myself, I couldn't help but wonder if they were planning on eloping anyways. I walked on eggshells around the family as long as I could remember and I longed to get away from White Oak.

When she finished, I asked, "Why did you let them stay?"

"I'd lost one daughter. I couldn't lose them both and Malery was just a baby. Where would they have gone?" Her voice distant, lost in memories.

"What about Grandpa? Didn't he try to stop it?" I asked. Where was he in all this?

She lowered her chin and pressed her cold lips against my cheek in a kiss. "That's a story for another day."

I spent that summer with Grandma and Miss. Dresdan. White Oak becoming a place that didn't harbor quite so many negative memories, but I never really trusted my grandma. I even wondered how much of the story she told me was true. Her words were all I had.

Grandma's Version

The red traced the pink and gold as the sun lowered on the horizon. In the perfect position, its reflection spreading across the placid surface, including us in its splendor. As if we were suspended inside it.

"Don't tell your grandma I poured in a dash of tequila," Miss. Dresdan said with a wink as she handed me a glass of sweet tea.

I giggled in disbelief that she spiked it.

She smiled. "This place has a beauty all its own. Don't you think?"

"Sure, I guess."

She turned her head from the sunset and studied me. "You've always been like the granddaughter I never had. Maybe, if--"

I knew what she was going to say. "Don't. You are a grandmother to me, more than my flesh and blood."

"Now you watch your words. That woman loves you. She's been good to you and me."

If she knew how she'd stuck me in the attic the day of my uncle's death she might think otherwise. My grandmother had always been good to Miss. Dresdan though. I bit my tongue, something else was going on. "Is Grandma OK?"

"Yes, yes, she's fine. You're always perceptive, so smart." She paused for a beat.

"I'm getting older and this work is getting to me. Such a big house. Your grandmother has given me a retirement, something your granddaddy set up before he passed." She held her spiked sweet tea with both hands, her gaze focused on the horizon.

I furrowed my brows. "What are you saying?" Worry clenched my gut.

"I'm moving to southwest Florida to one of those retirement communities where the residents play bingo every week. It's real nice."

Water threatened to leak from my eyes. I hadn't been gone a year and my life was dropping from under me. She was the rock in my life. The person always there for me. *How would I ever come back to White Oak?* "Will I ever see you again?"

"I hope so. I'm not dying. I'll give you my address and phone number before you return to school."

Some semblance of relief ran through me. She mentioned my grandfather. I wanted to know more, in case I never did see her again. "Tell me."

"Tell you what?"

"All of it."

She narrowed her eyes. "I hope you have all night. My life's been long but good, mostly. Hell, I still have years to go, crashing that retirement community." She smiled wide.

I gazed at her, brimming with expectation.

"Well, I guess I'll start when I wasn't much older than you. At fifteen I got pregnant with Arvid. His daddy ran out on me before he ever knew. It was better that way, so Arvid didn't have to get attached to him before losing him. My family was poor, real poor, and my baby and I were mouths to feed. In other words, I was kicked out."

I drew in a breath.

She continued her story. My granddaddy found her crying behind the ice cream parlor where she worked part-time. He brought her home and put her up in the same little house she's lived in all these years. He had people fix it up and modernize it.

He and my grandma offered her a job working for them, cooking, light house cleaning, and helping with the children. Grandma was pregnant with Alma, my mom. Arvid and Alma grew up more as brother and sister and were very close. That I already knew.

She continued to work for the family. The jobs changed over time, but she was always employed. She and Grandma became very close.

"What was Granddaddy like?"

"He was a beautiful man with so much love in his heart. He would have loved you to smithereens." She chuckled. "He was a good father, loved being a daddy."

"Why did Grandma step out on him?"

"You're treading spiteful waters. Your grandparents' marriage wasn't what it seemed, although, they loved each other a great deal."

Riddles, why did adults speak in riddles? "What do you mean?"

She placed a hand on my knee and her face became serious. "That's not my story. You'll need to ask your grandma but your mom and aunt were born into love."

My aunt wasn't too loving. "Thae why is Aunt Olivia such a bad apple?"

She chuckled. "A what? Bad apple? You mean bad seed? Well, sometimes those born with everything want more. They think they're entitled to it."

The next day, my bags packed, the driver loaded them into the trunk. I climbed into the back seat ready to start a new school year.

I worried about the school year and Johnie. I missed her even though we spoke every week. Her last call she remembered, telling me every detail of her traumatic memory. She was a baby, two or three maybe, and her father picked her up from daycare because her mom worked the night shift at the hospital.

They stopped for gas and he went inside to pay, parking the car right in front so he could see her, keep his eye on her so nobody would steal her. It was ironic that his concern was for her safety and he's the one...

A man with a ski mask appeared from nowhere. Somewhere, but for her, who was watching her daddy, nowhere.

He was just there with a gun in his hand. He pointed it at the cashier who instead of handing over the cash brought a gun from under the counter.

Her father was in the line of fire. He ran towards the door and the ski mask man shot him in the back then the cashier shot him and called the police.

The bullet hit her father in the head and because he shot from behind the blood splatter coated the door. He dropped a couple feet in front of it. Killed instantly.

She waited in the car for a long time before her mom got there.

Now that she remembered, she saw things more frequently with more control, and not only death. She touched her mom's wedding dress and saw the fun they had, laughter, kissing, and love.

I was happy for her and hoped one day to see her again. She promised me we would meet up when I least expected it.

She was going to a local private school and would be home every night.

Ella Louise wasn't a perfect school, but it wasn't White Oak. I was learning nothing in life was perfect, everything and everyone was damaged. Happiness could be found under the wreckage. One just had to pick up the pieces.

Lissa and Robin greeted me with hugs and Lissa's nonstop vocalizations about her summer break. How she flew to Japan by herself and spent most of the summer with her family there then flew home in time to take a cruise with her parents to the British Virgin Islands. I admired how well-traveled she was and wished it for myself. My life didn't compete with hers, as all I'd done is go back to White Oak and was pleased neither Malery nor my aunt were home.

Robin's life wasn't as exciting either but still she'd done more than stay home all summer. She had friends in her neighborhood and spent most days with them, and her family took a vacation to Disney where they stayed at a resort in Orlando.

I feared I'd never leave Louisiana and vowed to myself that day I'd leave like my mom. She ran with her secret lover and built a life that included three children and was even lucky enough when my daddy was killed to have Arvid who swept up the pieces of her and glued them together. Wonderment fluttering through my head, I wondered why I was left. Why hadn't I been killed like my parents and brothers? *Did the murderer not know I was there?*

The three of us spent so much time discussing our summers, well Lissa and Robin more than me since mine was boring compared to theirs, that we were nearly late for dinner. The new girls were trickling in. I caught Greta studying them with her cerulean blue eyes, small sideways glances. She hadn't said a word to me, hadn't even looked my way.

My heart ached. The day I untied her she'd been open and humbled. A different person than the one who sat across the room, studying the fresh meat. It was as if she entertained two personalities. Warm tears threatened my eyes and my nose started stuffing up.

Lissa, opposite me, leaned in close and whispered, "Do you think Greta will try initiation again?"

I hoped not. She promised me, but I'd never told anyone about that day. It was our secret.

"She'd be stupid after what happened last year. Sam was her best friend," Robin crooned.

The warning and sentiment in Robin's tone struck me with a sudden thought. The things Greta and I did, had she done them with Sam? *Were they those kind of friends? More than school friends, but kissing girlfriends?*

Lissa and Robin carried on a conversation I barely heard as I observed the cafeteria. All the groups in their usual spots with new girls sprinkled throughout until they found their place like the school was caught in a time warp. "Where do we fit?" I asked.

Lissa and Robin stopped talking and stared at me. "What do you mean?" asked Lissa, her face twisted in confusion.

"The jocks, the hoes, the nerds. Where do we fit?"

"Oh," Lissa responded.

Robin answered, "We're entitled, or at least that's what everyone says. Our families aren't upper middle class like doctors and lawyers, we don't have scholarships. We come from rich, powerful families who have empires."

I thought carefully about her words. Empires echoed in my brain. My grandma hadn't worked a day in her life. *Where did our family's money come from?* The agrarian plantation life died over a hundred years ago, most of the wealthy southern families who lived high on the knob in their fine houses with a multitude of slaves lost everything. *How had my family survived and made money in spite of the declining southern economy?*

After dinner, I was quick to escape the cafeteria but not quick enough as Greta walked past me, her arm and hand brushing against me as she shoved a note into my palm. Not once did she glance my way or acknowledge me as she focused on her friends.

Robin gave me a side-ways glance, her eyes zeroing in on Greta's proximity as she brushed past me. Once we got to our room she asked, "What was that about?"

Lissa glanced at her then me, as Robin's gaze was fixed on me. I unfolded my hand revealing the note. "I don't know."

A very confused Lissa insisted, "Open it."

It read, *Meet me North Tower, midnight.* Lissa and Robin were my friends. They were with me, listening in, during initiation, helping Johnie and I in New Orleans, yet I hesitated to tell them. The moment Greta and I shared was private, arousing desires I hadn't known existed. "Greta wants me to meet her later."

"Are you?" Robin inquired, a hand on her hip and stern expression across her face. They weren't the only students in the school who hated Greta and, as much as I wanted to and should have, I couldn't. My feelings for Greta ran deep.

Lissa bounced to the alcove. "You should. I told you my dad owns Mintech and he gave me new stuff. She dragged out a velvet bag. Inside it a necklace with a stunning ruby rose in the center. "This is a camera and it records sound. We'll hear and see everything." Her lips curled into a pleased smile.

What if Greta and I shared another moment? All the water in my mouth evaporated and I was instantly parched as I gathered spit and swallowed. Their expressions determined, helpful. They were being good friends. Reluctantly I took the necklace. "Show me how it works."

Robin sat on the edge of her bed, an expression of devastation on her face as Lissa showed and explained the device to me.

"What's wrong?" I asked Robin when Lissa took a short breather from talking.

Her finger twirling the bedspread, her eyes fixed on a spot or groove in the wooden floor said, "No one goes to the North Wing, not even the staff. It's said to be haunted."

"Pig spit," Lissa said as she laid the necklace on the chest. "This building is old and probably filled with spooks surrounding us all day, every day, but we don't see them. We demystified the entire story Greta tells. That woman didn't die here in childbirth to a black baby. I doubt there're really any ghosts. It's an old, large building. They don't need the extra space."

I blew air out of my cheeks. "I'm going. Maybe your camera will pick up on the spirits but I'm going to see what this is about."

After the teachers' head check Robin and Lissa curled onto Lissa's bed with a small handheld device that worked as a viewing screen. She said it was the phone of the future. I pressed the center of the rose as Lissa demonstrated.

The halls were dimly lit with small night lights, enough I saw my way. My feet padding over the wood floors the only noise disrupting the deafening silence. Shivers ran up my spine as I entered the north wing. Absent of night lights, I pushed the button on a small flashlight Lissa provided me with at the last minute and hurried down the hallway, moving fast to avoid spooking myself.

Closed doors lined the left and the right but I focused on neither as I kept my eyes in the beam of light that spread across the floor in front of me. I halted when I reached the ajar tower door. Moonlight spread, sweeping down the stairs and shone over my slippered feet.

Apprehensively, I pushed the door wide. "Greta," I called with no response as I lifted my foot to take the first step.

In that same moment a creak sounded to my rear. Blood pumped through my veins. "Greta, is that you?" Uneasily I turned on my heel, shining the light over the floor and walls.

A hand touched my shoulder and I jumped off the ground, falling backwards onto someone.

"Get off me," Greta said as she pushed my back. She giggled as I stood, pointing my flashlight at her.

"That was you, right?"

She pushed my hand that was shining the light in her face. "What?"

"I swore I heard a door open." I flashed my light over the hallway again.

"You're scaring yourself. Come on." She bounded up the steps shining her own flashlight.

The tower was filled with intricately hand carved furniture, over a century old I reckoned as I ran a finger along the dusty edge of a chair. Moonlight swathed the room, mingling with the dust gave it a hazy appearance. "What is all this?"

"It belonged to the Hartleys. I want to show you something." Greta halted by a large cypress chest and lifted the lid. Her flashlight illuminated a white dress, made of satin with lace trim.

Obviously, she'd already spent time in the North Tower. My eyes widened. "It's beautiful."

Carefully she tucked her arms into the chest and lifted the dress out. She held it up and pressed it against herself. "She was my size." She laid the dress over the chest and lifted her nightgown over her head, displaying her developing breasts. Enough moonlight shone inside the room to put their perky form on display. Pink nipples the size of quarters hardened at the ends.

Wetness unexpectedly coated my panties as I couldn't take my eyes from her perfect, chiseled breasts. I knew I shouldn't feel that way about her but my body spoke otherwise. Dainty lace panties covered her female privates.

I quickly glanced away but not before she caught my roving eyes. "You like what you see?" she asked, picking up the dress and stepping closer.

I didn't answer, my panties growing wetter. I swallowed as I helped her lift the dress over her head. She took my hand and guided it between her breasts. I yanked it away, remembering Lissa and Robin were on the other end, watching and listening.

"Turn around," I said.

She licked her lips. "I know you want me. I see it in your face." She slid a finger between my legs. "I feel it down there. You are so wet." She reached for my hand, holding the dress up with her other hand. I drew away. "Go on, touch it. I want you to."

I fought the urges developing inside me to rub myself against her, to feel her soft porcelain skin against my fingers. I swallowed and walked behind her, pulling the dress the rest of the way down and fastening it. It wasn't only that I didn't want Lissa and Robin to share a private moment between Greta and I, but we were both girls and it wasn't right.

She turned around, facing me. The silk dress flowing around her in a circle, her breasts showing above the lace trim. I stepped back and drank her in.

With the exception of her modern hair-style she was the spitting image of Ella Louise.

"What?" she asked, her blue pools narrowing.

"You... you," I stammered, "look like her."

She lifted the dress and walked towards a grouping of covered furniture, pulling the cover off revealed a mirror. Its wooden edges carved in complex designs. Letting the dress fall into place, she stared at herself, shifting to one side and smiling. "I do, don't I."

I glanced away and collected my thoughts. "Is this why you brought me here?"

She puckered her lips, kissing the air, then spoke, "No, this place is like stepping back in time. I think it would be perfect but I made a promise to you and it means something for me to keep that promise. I'd like to continue the time-honored tradition of initiation but change it up. I want to use this room."

She continued to explain how she wanted to keep the story going, and the worm, but since we were in the house she thought a Ouija board would be more appropriate to speak with the dead. The tower absent of electricity, the original sconces on the wall could be used. She flitted about the room with her ideas but the best didn't come until last. "I want you to help me, to be my right hand."

I scoffed. "What? No, it's a horrible idea!"

She pressed her hands against her hips, her blond hair shining in the moonlight. "It's a great idea and you know it. Everything will be safe and no one will leave this room until everyone leaves. Tell me at least you'll think about it."

She was persistent as a cowlick. "Fine, I'll think about it."

My Own Little Secret

Robin and Lissa, mostly Lissa, nearly assaulted me as I entered the room. "What was that about? She's a lesbian? I can't believe how she hit on you. Are you going to do it?"

I unclasped the necklace and handed it to Lissa. "She's all show. I don't think she's gay." I knew better as the words left my mouth but admitting she was, well it was admitting I was too and at thirteen I didn't think I understood enough about the complexities of emotions between couples yet to admit anything. Nor did I think Greta, at fourteen, knew much more than I did.

"Her breasts are larger than mine," Lissa noted, squeezing her nubs. Her eyes wandered over mine and Robin's chests. "I think your boobs are bigger than hers. I guess they weren't really big but smallish and full. They'll be big one day." Lissa gawked downward at her own in dismay. "I'll never have any. My mom doesn't either."

Robin chuckled at Lissa's talk and observance of our developing figures. "My mom says once I start my period mine will grow. She's a solid C cup. I hope mine grow that size."

Initiation was another beast to tackle. Sitting on the edge of my bed, I folded my hands together and rested them on my legs. "Greta does what Greta wants. She'll go through with initiation whether I consent, join her, shun her, or tell on her."

The walk back gave me plenty of time to consider my position. If I was there, as an equal, not her right hand like Sam, we could do it right. I'd make demands and take the precautions she threw to the wind. Robin and Lissa hung on my every word. "I'm going to do it but I have a few rules of my own that she'll have to follow."

They weren't stunned. Lissa let out a breath as if she was holding it, hoping I'd make the choice I did.

Robin, always observant and wise beyond her years, asked, "What did she mean about promising you?" It was impossible to get anything past her.

I told them about finding Greta tied to the tree and how I untied her, making her vow to never do initiation again. I left out how we kissed.

The next night, at the same time, I met Greta. I unclasped the rose camera necklace and dropped it beside the wall outside the door and closed the door behind me.

Greta waited, sitting cross-legged on the floor. She smiled expectantly.

I lowered myself, sitting across from her, drawing my knees to my chest inside my nightgown. "I'll do it but no one leaves alone and," I paused, "I'm not Sam, this isn't all about you. It's about me too and mostly the new girls."

Her blue eyes bubbled as she pushed herself forward, hands on the wood floor and kissed my lips. "Thank you!"

I drew back and she crawled forward, her lips again meeting mine in a kiss. I slipped my tongue through her parted lips and inside her mouth. Her tongue wrapped around mine brought back the wetness in my panties and the mysterious urges. I shouldn't feel them for her, but knowing that didn't stop our tongues from devouring the other's.

She climbed over me. I leaned back, lowering my head to the floor as she straddled me, our lips locked in a kiss. Our breathing heavier with each fervent, passionate moment. *Did this make me a hypocrite?* I'd used Malery's gayness as blackmail. I didn't approve of it, yet here I was lip-locked with Greta and relishing each second as my hands moved under her shirt and fondled her soft breasts that I'd wanted so much. The nipples hard and indulgent.

She moaned between kisses, then brought a hand to mine and wiggled my nipple between her pointer and middle finger. Lost in that moment we disregarded social norms and gave in to our desires. Maybe what we were doing was far more normal than we thought. Interest in sex wasn't uncommon for puberty, at least Miss. Dresdan told me that. She'd never lied to me.

Everything felt so good, my body shuddered in excitement as we lay on the floor next to each other. "This can be our secret place. The door locks from the inside." As if that was the reassurance I needed to accept her invite.

Whatever was between us was mutual but she didn't seem to feel the guilt I did. "I don't think we should. We're both girls."

She lifted up on her elbow. "It doesn't mean we can't see boys too. We experiment with each other, so we know what we're doing with the boys."

Is that what this was? An experiment? Isn't that what I'd already been thinking simply put in Greta lingo?

Initiation was pulled off the following Saturday night under my watchful eye and that of the eldest former Scraps. Under the hot plate Greta carried herself like a true Southern Belle, which I knew better. I understood who she really was beneath her layers of disguise.

It was the following day I caught a glimpse of myself in the mirror after stepping out of the shower. My breasts, like Lissa noted, were large and my butt was round and full. I sported curves around my waist and hips. I'd never seen myself through someone else's eyes.

My hair less unruly than in my younger years, curls spiraled down my back.

"What are you doing in there? I'm going to go gray if you stay in there any longer," teased Lissa as she knocked on the door.

I wrapped a towel around myself and opened the door. I widened my eyes in surprise. "Oh. No. No. Will you look at that." I pretended to pluck something from Lissa's head.

"Is it a bug? Get it off," Lissa screamed, jumping up and down.

I fell over laughing. "It's just a gray hair."

She struck me with a uniform blouse in her hand. "That wasn't funny." She giggled under her breath. "It wasn't," she repeated as we swapped spots.

Time flew fast. I longed for the days Greta and I stole away to the north tower where we dressed in the old clothes stored away up there and pretended to be ladies of the ball, dancing in the tight-waisted dresses that opened wide as we dipped and twirled. The wedding dress was my favorite on Greta. Its long train flowed behind her as she spun a parasol to the side.

Our imaginations put together a wedding to each other. We made vows and recited them.

"I take Debbie as my wife to have and to hold, forever and always," Greta declared as she took my hand in hers.

Cerulean eyes bright and filled with delight brightened her face.

"I take Greta for better or worse, for richer, for poorer, in sickness and in health, to love and eternally cherish." I slipped a cigar band around her finger that we'd found in one of the many chests scattered throughout the room.

We kissed, long and hard. In our world, anything could happen. A black woman could marry a white woman without conflict, without shame, without nasty looks and words from others.

The winter dance came. It was the only one the junior high girls were allowed to attend. Greta was a year older, in ninth grade, so she'd be able to attend the spring prom as well. Dressed in a full-skirted skater dress covered in sheer Victorian style lace I opened the door for Greta whose round eyes grew rounder. "Holy shit," she mouthed.

Robin and Lissa dropped what they were doing. "What is she doing here?" asked Lissa with a bite.

Greta's stare stung as she dropped a bag on my bed.

"I asked her. She's going to do my hair. If you like, maybe she'll do yours."

Lissa turned away and mumbled something that sounded like, "If you want her to fry it." They didn't like that Greta and I were getting close. We didn't make it obvious but Lissa and Robin caught on quick enough that I liked Greta. I'd given her a chance.

Robin dropped onto the edge of my bed. "I could really use someone to help with my makeup. I don't know the first thing about applying it."

Greta placed her hands on Robin's cheeks and tilted her head. "You have good cheek bones. We need to accentuate those, maybe some natural tones around your eyes to bring out the natural jade color."

Robin sat scared stiff as if asking for her help was abominable, then relaxed after Greta pushed past her, plugging in a fat curling iron with changeable settings that she spread over my chest.

She started with Robin while the iron heated up. Lissa made a few glances our way but continued to shift through her side of the closet, hangers clanked against hangers as she scooted clothes willy nilly. She came out several minutes later wearing a dark green baby doll dress. It showed off her natural medium skin tones and her tiny frame.

"Wow!" Greta said. "The dress is perfect. If you want, I could add just enough color to your face that every guy from Landsom will have their eyes on you."

Lissa pulled a brush through her hair in contemplation as Greta brought a mirror to Robin's face then pulled her ginger hair upward and gently pulled a couple of natural curls down around her cheeks. "What do you think?"

"I don't know what to say. I don't even look like myself."

"That's the idea. We're all girls here. It doesn't matter from day to day how we look, but tonight, when we meet the guys, we need to make lasting impressions, so they won't forget us. Will long for us." Her drawl syrupy-sweet and seductive. The tone she used with me during our passionate make-out sessions.

I took Robin's place as Greta toiled with my hair, pulling the iron through it until it was nearly straight. Her hands in my hair was a delight, exciting my female hormones. I coughed, all the product she sprayed filled the air and tickled my nose. She held the mirror in front of me. "What do you think?"

"No one's ever tamed my curls. It's… my hair… it's so long and I love it." I jumped off the bed and wrapped my arms around Greta. Maybe it was too much in front of others. I started to back away when she pulled me closer.

"I wish I could kiss you now but tonight we flirt with the boys," she whispered, her head turned away from Robin and Lissa.

Lissa finally consented to having Greta apply makeup. She was an Asian bombshell by the time she was finished. Greta retreated to her own room to prepare to meet the boys.

Beauty to Behold

The cafeteria was converted into a ballroom, or the once-ballroom was used as a cafeteria. White, silver, and blue garlands hung from the doorways, glittered snowflakes dotted the walls, blue and white lights blinked flowing from each chandelier to a hidden spot on the wall and pretty blue ribbons wrapped the backs of the seats spread on the outer rim of the room.

The room was completely re-formed and even prettier than White Oak the day Grandma threw the Christmas party. I shuddered at the memory, envisioning my uncle sprawled on the floor, blood leaking from his head.

Lissa, Robin, and I joined some of the other *entitled* girls at one of the tables. Light glowed from the sparkly-blue snowflake table toppers. Inside wasn't a real candle but a plastic, battery-operated one. If one didn't look inside to see they'd think it very pretty.

The boys, already there, feasted their eyes on us and every girl as they entered as if we were meat. Older boys and girls -- upperclassmen -- laughed and spoke amongst themselves, providing quick hugs and cheek pecks. The hoes were quite popular with the guys as they rarely took their eyes away as if remembering a secret moment shared in the woods or by Hartley stream.

I watched for Greta to make her grand entrance. She wouldn't tell me what she was wearing, nearly everything with her was an unknown.

"I think he's watching you," Lissa offered, tilting her head in the direction of a dark-haired boy.

It was difficult to tell what or who he was staring at under the dark flap of bangs that covered his downward-tilted face. His skin, like mine, wasn't really light or dark but something in between. I knew he wasn't mixed like me but with something else as his hair was floppier and his skin tones more tannish and not quite so chameleon.

I'd learned in the past year at Ella Louise that the world wasn't painted black and white as I'd been taught growing up by my vengeful aunt and abusive cousin. It was more shades of various colors, everything in between the spectrum and beautiful.

My mind drifting back to Greta who still hadn't shown. I hoped nothing unforeseen happened to her. I didn't notice when Lissa and Robin left the table until someone asked, "May I sit with you?"

I glanced up into a set of beautiful brown eyes plugged into an oblong face with a strong jaw. A snowflake cup in each hand. How Lissa knew he was looking my way under the hair would remain a mystery.

I didn't have much choice and had no idea what else to say. "Sure."

"Here." He set a cup in front of me. "Punch. Drink it now before someone spikes it." He winked. His face was dreamy, like I could fall into it and never come out.

"Thanks. I'm Debbie." I faltered.

"Gabriel. I haven't seen you at one of these before."

"This is my first. I started last year after the holidays." I raised the cup to my mouth and sipped. The tart, fruity juices mingled when they hit my tongue.

We talked a few more minutes before he asked me to dance. He stood at least a foot and a half taller than me, with broad shoulders. A part of me couldn't believe this more than handsome, but devastatingly attractive, guy was interested in me. He had to be sixteen or seventeen judging by the smooth-shaven face. The younger guys didn't have anything yet to shave.

The world stopped the moment Greta waltzed into the room in a blue velvet crush dress that flattered her thin curves. I barely noticed the guy on her arm.

"Friends?" Gabriel asked.

We'd stopped, rather I'd stopped, dancing. Embarrassed, I'm sure my cheeks flushed. "I'm sorry. Yes, we know each other. I wouldn't say we're good friends." We picked up dancing where I'd left off, doing my best to ignore her. Tonight, we paid attention to the boys and Gabriel, from what I could tell, was quite a catch.

"She's a card. Henry swears he's in love with her, always sneaking out, meeting in the woods."

My throat choked up and my heart plummeted, smashing onto the shiny ballroom floor. I held it together, swallowing my heartbreak and jealousy, reminding myself for the second time in the matter of a few minutes Greta and I couldn't really be together, shouldn't be together. It was wrong, practice for the boys. "She's quite something." I chuckled stiffly.

Next time Greta swirled into my view I noted Henry. A delightfully handsome boy with sparkling green eyes set inside black chameleon skin like mine. His winning smile and left cheek dimple could win the charms of any girl. I should be happy she'd found such an attractive young man but as the most beautiful girl in Ella Louise I wouldn't have thought otherwise.

"You should sneak out with her next time she does. I'll be there waiting," Gabriel whispered in my ear as we took a seat and small plates filled with hors d'oeuvres were handed to us.

My palms grew sweaty at the implication of meeting a boy at night, making out with someone besides Greta. The idea and desire should be natural, I told myself as I considered what his tongue would feel like in my mouth. *Would it be as soft and fluid as Greta's? Would his kisses be too wet or too dry? Would he slobber all over my face the way I'd seen people on TV do?* My mind spent the evening convincing myself my apprehensions were normal.

Loud, deafening winds and hard rain beat against the sides of our room, waking me from a solid, sound sleep. I jumped out of bed, panic in my gut as I raced to the window. Branches soared through the air carried on the wings of spiraling winds and the torrential downpour.

My mind immediately spun to Lissa and Robin who weren't in their beds. A commotion in the hallway, pounding feet, sobbing, and harried voices took me away from the window and to the door. I flung it open as girls, faceless girls, pushed through the halls. I forced my way into the frenzy that, like the turbulent weather, carried me with it towards the west wing.

Glass shattered as a branch the size of a small tree crashed through the thick window, pinning a dark-haired, fuzzy-faced girl to the ground. I dropped on my knees and cried in my hands, sobbing like a child. The winds and mayhem stopped. Uncovering my face, the hall was empty.

The lucid vision stayed with me for several moments as I gathered my bearings and returned to the room. Lissa and Robin safe in their beds. The night silent and absent of the chaos I witnessed. The thing about my visions was the lack of control, the absence of faces and place and time. It would happen, but there was no way to predict when.

Death, always death. The grim reaper's chore girl, I was. I wished he'd choose someone other than me to share his dirty secrets of death with.

I didn't tell anyone, including Marva, about my vision. I didn't see her quite as often as I used to when Johnie attended Ella Louise. Those days seemed like another lifetime ago when we tied the cryptic pieces of history together.

The first time Greta and I met after the dance it took all I had to pull myself together. I wanted to scream, fly into a rage, tell her I loved her. Instead I quelled the storm inside me and agreed to go with her to see Gabriel when she next went to meet Henry. I couldn't tell from her actions if she wanted me as badly as I did her.

"We should practice," she said, but I thought it a load of bull as she'd been secretly seeing us both for some time and was saturated in practice. She traced my face and neck as she drew her full lips to below my ear and dropped kisses, working her way down my throat and chest to the tips of my breasts falling out of my bra. They were growing so fast now I couldn't keep a size.

Like clay, I melted as her tongue and lips journeyed over my skin, tingles erupted from one spot as she moved onto the next. I pressed my hands along her sides and lifted her shirt. Fumbling my fingers under her bra, I smoothed my hands over her chest.

"Oh yes, I want my nipples in your mouth. Take them." She laid her head back as I pushed her bra fully over her breasts and tickled her nipples with my tongue. She always liked that, as breathy moans escaped her lips. I coddled a nipple with my tongue while gently rubbing my finger around the areola of the other.

I pushed her back and she lowered her torso to the floor, her tongue all over my nipples. "We should go... all the... way," she groaned as her hands slid under my nightgown and edged towards my panties.

I sat upright. "I don't think so." I swallowed hard, as it took every bit of courage and self-control to say that.

She rose up on her elbows. "Feel me." She took my hand, placing it against panties that were every bit as soaked as my own.

I shook my head.

Her round eyes fully opened then, as if waking from a dream. "I feel you too. You want it as much as I do and when we meet the guys what do you think they're going to want? I've never done it with anyone and Henry's pants are near busting every time I see him. I can't hold him off much longer and I... I want you to be my first."

Henry. It was about him. She was using me, my feelings toward her, manipulating the situation. I scooted off her. "Henry will have to wait then because I'm not ready." At thirteen, nearly fourteen, I wasn't ready, but more I was hurt that she was using me to learn tricks for Henry.

She sat up, wrapped an arm around my shoulders and scooted closer. "I understand. I do. I shouldn't have asked yet. It's just that I'm fifteen now and Henry will be seventeen soon. He's ready, always so firm. If I don't soon he'll think me a tease and never see me again." She rolled her head back. "I have to relieve him with my hand so he doesn't suffer from blue balls."

That seemed more like Henry's problem than mine. Never mind that I had no clue what "blue balls" were, nor was I going to ask.

The dark night was lit with little flying bugs and the sky clear. Stars and moonlight reflected on the dewy grass and Greta and I made our way to Hartley Stream.

Henry's face lit up as soon as he spotted Greta. Taking her in his arms, he twirled her and planted a kiss on her mouth. They didn't waste any time in venturing a little further into the woods.

Gabriel greeted me and we sat, talking for several minutes before he took my hand. "You are very beautiful and I long to kiss you but only if you want me to."

Greta's moans, her familiar pleasure moans, echoed loud in my ear. The most beautiful young man I'd ever set eyes on wanted to kiss me. He was polite and perfect. I forced Greta from my head as I moved my lips towards his. It wasn't awkward, but not nearly as natural as it had been with Greta. His tongue was pleasant enough, not too wet or intrusive but soft and gentle.

We parted, his serious brown eyes staring into mine. "That was incredible."

It should be after months of practice with Greta, I mused. I pressed my lips to his again, drawing my body closer to his. Other than kiss, he never touched my girl parts. He was a junior at Landsom, seventeen come spring, and was a little shocked when I told him I was only thirteen but he said, with timeless beauty like mine, age didn't matter.

On the way back, Greta took my hand. "We moved to the next level tonight," she said gleefully. "I sucked him until he came. It was all salty and creamy. I want to taste yours, I bet it's sweet."

As long as she and Henry were a thing I wasn't *going all the way* with her. I knew it was jealousy but I wasn't her toy and she couldn't play with my feelings that way. "Gabriel is nice, hotter than every girl's fantasy and I think we should stop practicing with each other."

"What?" She halted, her face distorted in confusion and hurt. "Why?"

"We both have guys and need to be with them."

She sighed and dropped her head. "Your first boyfriend and you drop me? I've been seeing Henry for over a year now it hasn't stopped me."

No, it hasn't. You've been playing us both. I knew that was a stupid thought. We couldn't *be* together anyways. "It doesn't feel right to me. I can't do it, not as long as I'm seeing someone." The pain in my words radiated through my heart and every blood vessel in my body. I knew I loved her, not Gabriel. I'd never love him or anyone as much as I did her. A part of me, larger than I admitted, was brimming with jealousy. She wasn't going to see both of us but have to make a choice which she did.

She pushed thick, blond tresses behind her ears. "You're right. There's this part of me that wants you so badly, more than Henry or any man and it's wrong. I know it is, but I can't help it." She shrugged her shoulders, her cerulean pools stabbing my heart over and over.

Every day was a struggle when I'd see her. We passed in the halls like ghosts, swept our eyes off each other in the cafeteria, only talking the nights we met the guys. I wondered, the many times we visited them, why we never ran across the hoes. If they were as prolific as rumored to be, I'd have thought even once, but mostly more than once, we'd have run across them.

No Longer a Secret

The school year ended and summer flew by. My days spent reading by the tree, my mind flopping like a fish out of water -- Greta then Gabriel, Greta, Gabriel. I did everything to break free from my thoughts. Summer flowed into fall, the seasons passed, Gabriel and I grew closer. As a freshman I was able to leave campus once a quarter. We loaded up on the bus, our roommates designated as partners and with a curfew to meet back at the bus, we explored various areas of New Orleans.

Gabriel, a senior with a car, always picked me up. He took me to extravagant restaurants with rules about silverware, and shopping. We visited museums as he loved art. He pointed out Lake Pontchartrain and Lake Borgne and we picnicked in Audubon Park where we saw more than birds but arched-winged cattlehearts -- butterflies with white spots on their forewings and red on their hindwings.

Always, he dropped me off a couple blocks from the bus, Lissa and

Robin waiting. Lissa said 'we live vicariously through you' as I told them the fabulous stories about all the places and things we did. Together, I lived a false life, one I'd longer for. I was a belle. He took care of me, never once did I have to spend a dime my grandma sent, so I saved it up, stuffing it in Ella Louise's empty drawer inside the mausoleum.

Graduation was approaching and Gabriel would soon be going home then on to college. I accepted our relationship would soon end. Greta slipped me a note in the halls during class exchange. My heart leapt with mixed emotions as I read it. She asked me to meet her in the north wing at midnight, as always.

My brain and heart filled with disquiet, I made the choice to meet her. I had to. Every part of me missed her even though I adored Gabriel, or more what Gabriel represented, and his relaxed attitude. Greta was who I wanted, who I loved.

Her face serious as she lowered herself to the floor. "Henry and I have set a date before he graduates to... you know. To be honest, I can't stomach sucking his dick and swallowing his salty cum anymore. Sex has to be easier and more pleasant." She took my hands in hers. "I meant it when I said I wanted you to be my first. We should share that special moment in our lives because... I'm in love with you."

Words stirred in my throat but my vocal chords froze, stopping them from coming out. She said the words I'd waited so long to hear yet I couldn't get my own words out.

Her bright eyes darkened as she gazed at me in anticipation. "Debbie..."

Greta's words stung like a sweet-sharp candy cane. My vocal chords loosened and the words came out. "I love you and I've always wanted to lose my virginity with you."

She smiled wide putting her straight white teeth on display. As if the distance between us never happened, our lips meshed together in a long, open-mouthed, zealous kiss. When our lips parted for air we rested our noses together.

"I was hoping you'd say that. I got us something." From a decorative bag she pulled out something. I'd never seen such a thing before. It was shaped a little like a banana but it wasn't yellow. It was pink and the top appeared to wear a helmet.

"What is that?"

She giggled. "It's a dildo because we don't have cocks and it has different speeds and movements."

That's going inside me? was all I could think as she pulled something else out of the bag -- a little bottle of oil. I wasn't so sure about the toy and oil as she explained, but I was sure about her and what we were about to do. I may not be Henry but I would be her *first* and she mine. That had to mean more than being a man sporting a penis any day.

She lit some of the candles left there for initiation and we spread a blanket over the floor as we apprehensively laid down on it. Our lips and hands found each other, roving the soft familiar hills and valleys until they found the secret spot we'd never previously journeyed.

She pushed my panties down, caressing and relaxing me, while excitement bubbled inside me. Between kisses to the insides of my thighs she said, "I'm going to pleasure you first, relax, tell me, talk to me so I know what feels best."

I thought the dildo would hurt but, as she slowly worked it in, my body welcomed it. The sensations were overwhelming. My hormones fluttered. I wanted more but as soon as she went a little deeper it pinched. My moaning jarred into a slight scream.

"I'm sorry, I'm sorry," she apologized, worry written all over her beautiful face.

I let out my breath. "Keep going. It stung but it still feels incredible." After that initial prick that felt like needles poking my vagina it went away and I was intoxicated with so much pleasure the sensation was the most incredible euphoria as my body quivered with its release.

"That's my girl," Greta said as she slid up my naked body and covered my face with kisses.

I pushed her over. "It's your turn." Ever so gently, carefully, I gave her the same pleasure she'd given me until her body rocked with gratification as mine had.

We lay together, wrapped in each other's arms, until the first light of dawn.

We parted and hurried back to our rooms. I opened the door with a squeak and laid in my bed, pulling the covers to my chin as I fell into a dreamless sleep.

"Where were you?" Robin asked as Lissa departed to the restroom for a shower.

"What do you mean?" I was thorough as always and quiet, she couldn't know anything but still my heart skipped a beat.

A grim coating filmed over her jade eyes. "Last night. I woke up, you weren't here."

"I couldn't sleep so I walked the halls. I do that sometimes. I'm sorry if I woke you," I said in a steady voice hoping she bought my utter lie.

She shrugged. "You didn't wake me."

She never said another word but the tone in her voice gave me the impression she was aware of my night absences.

Granddaddy

efore we left for the summer, Gabriel, under the moonlit night, handed me a small box. Inside it was a gold ring with shiny red gemstone flower. It was so extravagant, yet simple and beautiful. "It's an amaryllis," he'd said, "because it's my favorite color and the flower represents pride and priceless beauty."

I accepted the ring. As soon as it touched my skin two lights shone into my eyes, blinding me. A screech filled my ears and ended with a thud.

"Thank you," I answered and followed with a kiss. My sight didn't need a specific medium to work. It came and it went as it pleased so it was the ring or the grim reaper's sick humor?

"It's a promise ring, because I promise myself to you. You are worth waiting for." His dark silk eyes read sincerity, but a shade of guilt swept over mine for carrying on with Greta and letting him think I cared for him. He was the right gender and that's why I stuck with him and the way he spoiled me so.

Guilt mixed with joy riddled me. Why was life so full of complex emotions of the heart? I hadn't waited for him. I gave myself to Greta. At the same time, I'd possibly marry and have children with Gabriel one day, not Greta.

He gave me his cell phone number and we kept in touch that summer as I spent the languid days anticipating life in school the following year without him. After our special moment, Greta and I hadn't met, nor would we. Together we lost our virginity, something no one else could ever have but men had to come before our desire for each other. "My parents would never understand," she admitted and neither would my grandmother, or so I thought.

I strolled into the house, a quiet conversation coming from the living room. At first I thought it was the TV, until I neared realizing it was my grandmother.

"I paid for your round-trip ticket, paying for your hotel, including room service. You have an expense-paid trip to Paris. Most children wouldn't be so spiteful as you..." Her words burned with anger. "Your sister! How dare you say her name?!" The phone clicked, followed by discreet sobbing.

I rounded the corner.
"Grandma... what's wrong?" Her dark eyes tired and hollow. So very pretty in her youth, lines and wrinkles creased her aging face and she looked worn down, ragged.

She cleared her throat and blinked back the tears. "Nothing, Debbie." A fake smile painted across her face.

This grandmother I'd first had little opinion about, then admired her as my savior, then hated her for betraying me. Now, years older and a bit wiser, I saw her through different eyes. She'd lost one daughter and the other had spent her life as a leech, sucking money and life from her. This small, crumpled woman was too proud to admit the failures she felt.

I placed my arm around her middle and hugged her and thought maybe if she remembered the good times they would overpower the bad. "You promised me a couple summers ago the story of you and Grandpa . Can you tell me now?"

She held my arm against her chest. "You are your mother's daughter." A tiny smile slipped across her face. "Your granddaddy. That is quite a story. I loved that man, but then it wasn't proper for a white woman with southern money to date a black man. So I married Patrick. You see, he had a secret too -- he enjoyed the company of men and so our marriage was one of convenience. From the outside we looked like a proper southern family. Inside, I had my lover and he had his."

I lifted my head from her shoulder. "But you had my aunt?"

"In the early days we tried sex. We had to make it look real, and a child did just that. She always had a nasty temperament. Born with it. I did love Patrick, but not as a proper husband. When Olivia grew older she hated your mother. Always jealous of her. Alma was a special girl, so bright she gave the sun a run for its money and everybody saw it. When Olivia's husband noticed Alma he made passes at her. I think that's why she ran. Had I known sooner, I'd have kicked that man out of the house. I hired a private detective who found her in Pensacola married to a man I didn't recall as a suitor." Her voice and eyes far away, suspended in time.

"They had two boys. I went to visit. When I heard they were killed and you were alive I had to bring you here. Shortly after, I fell sick. I can't apologize enough to you. The horrible things they must have done."

I wasn't sure her story made complete sense, after all wasn't it she who said someone came home with my mom that day, rescuing her from the clutches of my uncle? Maybe it was Miss. Dresdan, or maybe I didn't remember it correctly. It was even more possible and probable my grandmother didn't remember it properly.

My aunt was a spiteful person. She nailed that and the mention of her mysterious illness triggered another thought that I hoped wasn't true. Could my aunt be as mean as my mind was piecing together? "What was your sickness that kept you bed ridden for years?"

"I reckon the doctors didn't rightly know. One of those things I guess." The seed planted, my brain edged toward my aunt having something sinister to do with it so she could torment me -- her sister's only living child.

"My father was smart with money. He sold the family business and invested in the stock market when times were good. He was the fifth-wealthiest man in America. He accumulated so much it could never be spent in our lives and so much of it is still collecting dividends and interest. I never understood most of that. He threw the most marvelous parties and always invited William -- your biological grandfather -- to play piano. He was a very talented pianist. His hands worked magic with those keys and I lost myself. It was love at first sight."

She continued her story, filling my mind with all her fond memories of my biological grandfather and then she admitted that her father knew about the affair. He didn't say it in words, but actions, and she wondered if her father didn't have a secret of his own. She never did know as her parents were killed in a train crash.

It broke her heart into a million pieces. She was the only heir to a massive fortune. Patrick never wanted any of it. He was amused to call her his wife and was so in love with their children, both Alma and Olivia. He loved fatherhood and never cared any less for the daughter who wasn't biologically his. He passed away when Alma was fourteen from an AIDS related illness. "People didn't know about it, understand it, then. There was no cocktail of medications. He came down with a cold, turned into pneumonia, and without the white blood cells to fight it his body withered into nothing," were her exact words.

That wasn't the end of the sad, tragic path her life was to follow. William, my biological grandfather, became ill at nearly the same time. She was so involved with Patrick as he was her husband. She doted on him, had nurses in and out of the house and spent as much time with him knowing he wouldn't live much longer. The guilt ate her up, the quiver in her voice said so. After the funeral she saw William one last time. He was in so much pain, cancer had eaten up his body. His strong arms she adored wrapped around her became thin sticks. She laid her head beside him and held his hand as he said his last words, "I love you and Alma so very much." He breathed his last.

My mind wondered if the visions I had of the couple in the houseboat were really my mother or were they my grandmother and her lover? So much time passed since I experienced them, and faces were always fuzzy in them, it was hard to tell. They were visions that weren't death but love, although people in them were dead. I'd nearly forgotten about them. Maybe I wasn't under the grim reaper's thumb but, as Marva suggested, I needed to relive some violent tragedy in my past to gain control over this silly *sight* that was anything except a gift.

My grandmother's world shattered into so many small, indistinct pieces as she mourned both the men she loved. My mother knew her father, not as her father, but as a friend of her parents. Tears leaked from my eyes as I began to understand all the pain and loss my grandmother had endured in her lifetime.

"I'm so sorry, Grandma. I wish I could bring it all back."

She leaned her head on mine. "I thought I'd grow old together with my men but it wasn't meant to be, both dying so young like they did and at the same time, but I have you, Debbie, because of them. I thank them both every day."

Last Will and Testament

My grandma's confession was more than recalling her life. It was like a last will and testament. Over the days following she explained how the plantation once farmed sugar cane but, with her granddaddy envisioning the end of slavery and the monarchies of white men, started making rum from the sugar cane. He was just a boy but understood enough to know people like alcohol and there'd always be a need so he hired a few men and started a company -- Tradewinds.

The company grew and by the time prohibition started in the late 1920s, before she was even born, her daddy was the biggest supplier of illegal moonshine in Louisiana. Hidden in the bayou, and Louisianans, stubborn folk who like to celebrate big, he was never caught and made a fortune until the market became saturated and the stock market crashed. Two separate things she assured me. He'd accumulated enough wealth it got the family through and when prohibition ended his business was back on top of the legal market. "People no matter how dire the circumstances always turn to spirits," she assured me.

Her story and explanations of how moonshine was made brought back my own memories of the secret room. *Should I tell her? Show her?* I didn't know, whilst I wrung my hands together in deciding what to do. It wouldn't change anything for her to know but maybe it would provide her some level of comfort or…

"Grandma."

She glanced my way. Her dark eyes pools of sorrow from our trip down memory lane. "Hmm…"

"Would you like a refill of sweet tea?" I couldn't take her further down the dreaded past, sometimes it was meant to stay there.

The car turned up the wide, circular drive surrounded by waist-high hibiscus in an array of colors ranging from yellow to red, towering white oaks branched above touching the limbs as if holding hands. What had come to be a familiar sight, finally felt like home. A place I was part of, leading me into a bright future.

It wasn't more than a couple weeks into my sophomore year that Ms. Timble pulled me from class. In the far reaches of my mind I knew something awful was afoot but I didn't imagine even then what horrors would roll off Ms. Timble's tongue.

The door to her office open, I stepped inside, curious what I'd possibly done so wrong to be called on. What punishment awaited me? She faced the window that gave views of the courtyard with its high branchy trees that shaded nearly the entire space. Water spilled from the fountain dead set in the middle. Without turning around she said, "Take a seat, Debbie."

My gut overflowing with apprehension as her words sounded so grim, I took a seat across from her desk in the wide leather chair.

She turned, her face awash with gloom, her eyes deep, melancholy pits. She sat, her back straight as a board as she always carried herself well, folding her hands upon her desk she said the most devastating words. My ears wanted to shut them out, my vocal chords wanted to scream, but my body froze in shock, grief, and terror.

"Your grandmother passed away last night."

The water continued to flow from the waterfall, birds chirped in the air, outside the walls of her office everything was cheerful but inside me a storm brewed and bubbled like lava, waiting to erupt. One small, meek word from a voice I didn't at first recognize as my own asked, "How?"

"A massive coronary in her sleep. She died instantly." Ms. Timble stood then and came around the back of my chair. She placed her arms around my neck and held me.

A car came for me that afternoon to haul me back to White Oak for the funeral. My mind a flurry of thoughts, one that brought back the nightmare of my childhood -- my aunt and Malery, who'd surely be there. *What of my life now? Would I have to go back and live there under my aunt's thumb?*

It was dark by the time the car reached White Oak. I took a deep breath, filling my lungs with the muggy, still air before entering the house. The door creaked open on my command and the silence of the house resonated in my head. I didn't search for Malery or my aunt as I headed straight to my room and locked the door, dropped my bag on the floor, and fell onto my bed, crying into the crimson comforter.

A creak of the floor alerted me someone was walking in the hallway and stopped outside my door. I pulled myself into a seated position, shadowy feet stood on the other side of my door. The knob didn't turn at all and the shadow moved on. My aunt or Malery, I didn't know which, but moved my chest of drawers in front of the locked door, worried she had a key. Neither of them was getting in without my knowing it.

The next morning, as if the weather mirrored my emotions, dark clouds loomed in the sky. I left my room, scouting the hall first. Noting it was empty, I ran to the restroom. I didn't plan on leaving my room for any other reason until the funeral.

The creak in the floor and shadow between the bottom of the door and the floor reappeared, followed by a voice, "Debbie." My aunt's cold, harsh tone sent chills up my spine. I hadn't seen her in years. My grandmother had made sure of that, sending her away each summer and holiday when I returned. She'd paid my aunt to disappear and now the wretched woman stood outside the bathroom door.

"We need to talk, Debbie."

I gathered my strength as I flushed the toilet and washed my hands. *Be strong, be strong,* I repeated in my mind as I placed my hand on the knob. A dripping sounded from a faucet, assuming I hadn't turned the faucet on the sink all the way over I glanced over my shoulder. *Drip, drip, splash,* continued but not from the sink. I sucked in a deep breath, sure I didn't really want to look, and slowly turned my head towards the bathtub.

Crimson water flowed over the side, spreading across the floor towards me. A bony, thin, wrinkled hand dangled over the edge. I swallowed. *Whose death was I seeing?*

The water edged closer to my feet. In a hurry to escape the vision before it swallowed me, I twisted the knob in my hand and ran into my aunt. I'd forgotten she was there. Her hard, mean eyes glared at me.

Her hair loose, falling over her shoulders and breasts, more attractive than the tight bun she used to always wear. Small wrinkles surrounded her eyes and deep grooves cut through the skin on her forehead -- worry wrinkles -- what I'd heard them called. Her face pinched and absent of a smile or expression other than hate. "What do you want?" I asked, my voice every bit as frigid as hers.

"Is that the way you greet me, after all the years we've been apart?"

"What do you want?" I repeated.

"I see you're as stubborn as the old woman." Her eyes narrowed. "Regardless of how you feel about me, I am your aunt and I do care about you." Her hands pressed against her long skirt and thighs as the words left her mouth.

Rage, anger, hate, and darkness consumed me. A strength welled from somewhere inside that dark place. "Care! You care! Pulling me by my hair, my ears, telling me I was less than human because I'm half black, making me eat your scraps, hiding me away from the world, allowing your son to kick me, my legs in a constant state of bruises, and throw dirt in my eyes, call me all sorts of names. That's how you care!" Each accusatory step I took, she took a guilty one backwards until she was pressed against the wall.

"You don't understand--"

I cut her off: "What don't I understand? You hated my mother because she was a better person than you, because she escaped this wretched place, because she found love. Because she had Grandma's love. So that gave you the right to abuse and neglect her only living child."

Her pinched face drawn back, body flat against the wall, she didn't utter another word as I walked to my bedroom and shut the door. I wasn't coming out until the funeral tomorrow. I'd pee in my trashcan if needed. A few minutes later her footsteps receded downstairs.

It was hours later, the gloomy clouds still hanging in the sky, full of water but not yet ready to release the downpour, when a knock on my door and a familiar voice carried my thoughts from gloom to happiness. I flung the door wide and wrapped my arms tight around Miss. Dresdan.

She pulled me tight in a hug and let me cry on her shoulder. I was every bit her height now. After several minutes we moved to my bed.

"I'm so sorry, Debbie." She smoothed the matted spirals from my face. "Your aunt says you refuse to leave this room. There's a tray of food outside your door. Should I bring it in?"

"No." I shook my head. "It's probably poisoned like she poisoned Grandma"

"Sweetie," she pulled my head towards her chest, "she didn't die of poisoning but of a heart attack. It was the maid who found her the following morning. Your aunt wasn't even here, she was on a shuttle from the airport."

I talked into her chest. "I don't mean her death but all those years when I was small. She poisoned her so she could torment me. The child of the sister she hated."

"Your aunt treated you wrong, taught your cousin to treat you wrong, and there was bad blood between her and Alma, but poisoning? That's harsh even for her. Sibling rivalry, that's normal." Her words did little to convince me my despicable aunt had nothing to do with Grandma's mysterious illness that suddenly came on when I came to live at White Oak.

"Can I stay with you in your cottage, please? I can't stay here with them," I pleaded, my eyes begging her.

"Of course you can."

I was sure to lock my door upon leaving.

A knock on the cottage door that evening carried Miss. Dresdan and I out of our conversation. With curiosity, she opened the door to a middle-aged man in a dark suit and magenta tie. His gold hair slicked back, tan, square-rimmed glasses around his green eyes, and a solemn expression pasted on his semi-handsome face.

"Miss. Dresdan wonderful to meet you. I'm Elijah Alexander, Ms. Holstead's lawyer, may I come in?"

She opened the door wider for him to enter. His eyes searched the small cottage, finally focusing on me. "Miss. Chargois, it is a pleasure to meet you."

Miss. Dresdan insisted he sit and offered him a glass of sweet tea. His eyes shifting away but always coming back to me. "Ms. James told me I'd find you both here, said you refused to stay in the home Miss Chargois?"

I didn't speak. I couldn't imagine any reason a lawyer of my grandmother's would need to see me.

"What is your business with Debbie?" Miss. Dresdan asked with a to-the-point tone.

"First I must offer my condolences. Ms. Holstead," my grandmother, "was a client of ours. Our families have worked together for generations." Neither of us responded so he continued. "According to her last will and testament there will be a reading of it one month from the day of her death.

Miss. Chargois, she insisted, no that's not the right word. She was adamant you be there. Miss. Dresdan," his eyes shifting from me to her, "you are also a part of it. Both of you should be there. It will take place at my office in Baton Rouge."

He handed us both a business card. "Miss. Chargois--"

"Debbie," I finally said, tired of being called by my last name.

"Debbie, you will continue your studies at the Ella Louise School for Girls. A car will pick you up and drive you to my office. The arrangements were prepared in advance by your grandmother. I can't say any more about the will or what she left either of you but, Debbie, she loved you and I can say you are well provided for since the day she learned you were coming to live with her. She modified her will immediately."

His words left an eerie echo as he stepped outside into the cloudy darkness without a single shining star.

The only familiar faces at the funeral were the lawyer, Miss. Dresdan and my horrible family -- Malery and my aunt. All the other people were nameless faces in a crowd. I had no idea she knew so many people or that they would venture to the nether reaches of the Bayou to watch her casket lower into the ground. Most of them showed yesterday evening after I left the house for Miss. Dresdan's, worried the roads would get washed out with rain as the black clouds counted their moments to drench us in something torrential. They all stayed at the house.

I felt his foul eyes on me as Malery cast me a glare, his eyes quickly shifting away when he knew I caught him. I wondered if he had the silly voodoo doll in his jacket pocket where his hand rested and if he was poking it right now wishing all kinds of terrible things on me. They say time heals wounds but nobody says those wounds don't pop right back open.

As the coffin finished its final leg and met the soft earth, the first raindrop hit my umbrella, rolling off, another, then the clouds opened up and the deluge nearly washed us out as everyone scampered back to the house, running through the mucky ground, umbrellas doing little to shield any amount of the rain as the winds blew it sideways, twisting the feeble wires.

Miss. Dresdan looped her arm through mine as we walked, not ran, back to the house. With her near and so many strangers I wasn't in danger, although I was more than hesitant to eat any of the food and chose to wait until that evening at Miss. Dresdan's.

People greeted me, offered me their condolences and deep regrets, but even upon their introduction they meant nothing to me, former relations of some sort to my grandmother. Tired of the barrage of people, I headed out of the parlor towards the front door when Malery stopped me.

He'd grown so tall, towered at least a foot and a half above me. His frame was slightly bulkier than the last time I'd seen him but he was still very thin and wore a mustache now. He sauntered closer to me, standing between me and the door. "I hated you, truly hated you, but there's a fine line between love and hate and it was Grandmother who made me hate you so. It was also Grandmother I owe for my life now. She paid for my college even though I wasn't worthy of a private education like you and was forced to attend public schools. She paid for the university and my degree. I have a good job, and I'm closing on my first house in two weeks."

I stared into his eyes, throwing daggers, and the lava inside my heart seeped into my veins, viscous and thick. The air between us silent, he continued.

"Even before you were a part of my life, Grandma did nothing special for me, never a trip anywhere, no gifts, not even a game or a special moment between us, but you, she adored you, dressed you in little frilly dresses and shiny patent leather shoes. You looked like a doll. The animosity between my mother and our grandma developed into something worse. A disdain for one another that runs deeper than the roots of the cypress you always laid under. It's blacker and murkier than the placid waters. Which gives us common ground. We are more alike than I think you realize."

I furrowed my brows, holding my stance, arms folded across my chest in defiance. "We are nothing alike!"

"Cousin, we are. You see, we lived in that hate-filled world, we learned to hate just as they did. We were both prisoners of a tragedy that happened before either of us was born. We also both escaped. My mother is a bitter woman who will die in this house, alone, like her mother did and we will continue our lives always shadowed by the darkness of this house and land."

I considered his words which were beginning to sound something like an apology, Malery-style, only I never heard him apologize for anything, ever. "What are you saying?" I wanted to hear the words not his confession.

"I'm saying be free of the White Oak shackles, live your life remembering no more the pain this place brings. I'm not saying I won't ever stop hating you. A part of me will always wish the ground would swallow you whole even though I know I shouldn't hate you. That's why I'm telling you to run, escape this. Don't ever look back." He moved to the side allowing me passage to the door.

"I'll see you in hell." I swung the door open and absconded into the dark, starless night. Rain cascading over my face and clothes.

Something on the X Chromosome

I had the *touch* yet it never once showed me things I wanted to see, only death, and not my grandmother's. It provided me no warning. I decided it was time to take control, whatever evil I had to relive and suffer would be worth the clarity of vision and control over such a skill.

Marva, like in the days with Johnie, sat in the little wooden chair at the table in back of the cabin. Surprise lit up her eyes when she spotted me. I wasn't greeted with hugs as I'd hoped, but with scolding, upset I'd stopped coming around, especially since I still had many dark layers to unravel.

In the cabin, no light except the scented candle, Marva helped me but, like previously, only small clues were revealed. The blurry man with the bloody knife and a low rumble. It became louder the more I focused on it until it sounded like I was standing beneath a massive waterfall. It encompassed me with a taciturn foreboding. My eyes popped open and my fast breaths slowed to normal.

Marva's kind face and eyes caressed me in warmth.

"Will I ever get past it?" I asked her.

"Trauma isn't something your brain wants to relive that's why it finds a way to bury the memories. Your gift is so different than most girls. Sugar, I've never seen anything quite like it."

Girls, always girls which begged the question, "Are guys ever touched?"

She chuckled. "No, not that I've ever heard of. You see there's something in those what-ya-call-its on that extra X chromosome we got that makes us the superior of the species."

I giggled, hardly believing that was it. When I stopped laughing my face grew somber. "Ella Louise's body isn't in the mausoleum."

Her brows made a V. "What brings that up?'

I shrugged. "I checked. There isn't even a death certificate."

She scratched her neck thoughtfully and stared out the little window. "No, I suppose there's not. What brings this up?"

I turned my eyes down and stared at the ends of the crocheted blanket beneath me. "I'm not sure. It's like something I think I need to know and I don't understand why."

She gave me an understanding nod. "Claiming and exercising your *touch* is a tricky process and, as I've said, you have many layers." She paused for a beat. "Do you want to know what really happened those many, many years ago?"

I nodded.

"I think there's a way for you to know." She stood and opened the door for me to follow. "I'm not sure how it will help you except it's focused practice."

We journeyed through her chunk of land to a clearing with slabs of rock covered in hand carved words that looked as though a child did them. "This is their graveyard, not the rich, white Hartleys but my family and others like them. This ground holds the answers you seek. All you need to do is let the spirits in so they can guide your mind."

She made it sound so much easier than it was. I walked between the markers, attempting to feel their energy and hear their stories. I laid my back against the ground, sifted the dirt through my fingers. Marva watched from the edge of the graveyard. I closed my eyes. Many minutes passed and I didn't think I was doing anything right.

"Relax, open your senses. Let them speak to you," Marva's voice soothed me and melted the tension.

My muscles slackened, my breathing steadied until my body was somewhere between asleep and awake. It was that moment in between when flames climbed high into the sky. Commotion, indistinct chatter, and loud, pounding footfalls like someone, no, more than one person, a few people were running.

My mind journeyed through the fire into an empty cabin. Whispers spun around me. "You must go tonight, go now, through the woods." A young, colored woman, a head rag covering the top of her head. Her face unclear. "He's coming." Three other hazy figures exited through a back door, sprinting into the woods, the darkness swallowing them.

The indistinguishable figures cleared as Mr. Hartley with his rugged good looks, sporting a beard, staggered towards the cabin with a torch. "Bastard! My wife is ruined! You're lower than the cow, at least it provides food. You..." His rambling continued as he rocked on unsteady feet. The torch waving all directions until he tossed it at the tiny cabin. The fire caught quick as flames licked the sides, moving to the roof until the fire swallowed the tiny house in an inferno.

"Put out that fire! Now!" he said, blundering on his feet.

Colored people rushed into action, hauling buckets of water, tossing the water onto the little cabin until the last of the flames was dead. The cabin destroyed, burned to the ground.

A series of captured moments told the rest of the story. Mr. Hartley bedding the young, colored girls, using them as his personal harem. Ella Louise catching a glimpse, her face twisted in disgust with an edge of satisfaction. A light-skinned baby lay in a basket, sleeping.

Ella Louise tending an injured colored man herself, cleaning a gash in his leg and wrapping it. Next, his strong, thick, muscular arms held Ella Louise tightly to his bare chest. Her dress hiked up over a worktable. Her arms draped around him as she moaned in pleasure.

The flashes smoothed out, rolling into a video. Ella Louise knew all along what her husband was -- a male whore. She hated him even though, at one time, she worshipped the ground he walked on, thinking him a true southern gentleman. She became pregnant, unsure whose it was, her husband's or the slave's.

She dropped the worm into her husband's wine after she'd coated it with something syrupy like honey, knowing how heartedly he drank at dinner, counting on it. As soon as the liquid hit his mouth, he grabbed his throat as if choking then his lips turned blue and his head dropped onto the table, his forehead hitting his plate. He hadn't died of choking, she killed him with an allergic reaction.

Over the next few months her belly swelled and she stayed out of public sight as a grieving widow. When her water broke she called a colored midwife, who birthed all the children on the plantation, to deliver the baby. Her pain and blood-curdling screams wracked me with shivers as the baby was finally born. Small and ashy, he was most definitely not her late husband's.

She handed him to a couple who her husband deemed worthless, as they couldn't have children of their own, promising to take care of them always, and the baby, so long as they claimed she died in childbirth. She fled Ella Louise Plantation.

My eyes popped open and I sat upright, breathing heavily, my hands planted on the ground behind me.

"Did you see what you needed?" Marva inquired; her voice smooth.

"What happened to her after she fled?"

"They didn't show you that?" She let out a deep breath. "Well, she went back north to her family and tricked her dying father into buying the plantation and assigning her head mistress for the Ella Louise School for Girls. When she returned to the area as Emmalane Pierce it had changed so much, high society temporarily suspended, no one recognized her. The end of the civil war and slavery brought the south to its knees.

"To ensure her privacy, she wore floppy hats and veils for each season, claimed her skin was too sensitive to the light. All of it lies of course but she did hire the couple who kept her baby as their own. He spent at least part of his life here working for her. Far as I know, he never knew she was his mother."

Ella Louise's story brought me back to my own. *Who was I really? What dark history was hidden in the stones of White Oak, buried beneath the murky water of the bayou?*

Greta knew something of the story, maybe Marva had taken her to graveyard as she had me, but Greta twisted it to fit her needs. I didn't have time for her nonsense and as much as I wanted her to hold and comfort me I didn't go to her, instead I called Gabriel. He was full of energy as he described college life. I envied him.

We met soon after in the lobby of a grand hotel in New Orleans. Lavish chandeliers and marble floors with couches and tables spread into small private areas between statues and beams. He looked like a million dollars but he wasn't the everyday college boy. His family had money and didn't spare a penny with him. Our hands entwined, we entered a large suite. The frame of the bed a rich gold color with off-white, succulent padding on the headboard and rich burgundy drapes over the windows. My mouth gaped.

"I have another surprise for you," he said, his face lit up like all the stars at night. He handed me a box from the bed-matching, gold-trimmed table. Inside was a red, see-through negligee with a matching cover. It was no surprise what he wanted and was ready, but was I? I hadn't told him about my grandmother, with no good explanation why. I told myself I didn't want to depress him with my sadness and other pitiful excuses.

Words stumbled from his mouth, my ears hearing bits and pieces. "I'm in college... I can't wait forever... It's you I want, but temptation is strong..."

I kissed his lips to shut him up. He took that as a yes.

The negligee in my hands, I stared at my body in the mirror. *Did I really want this?* A part of me did, the messed up, sorrowful wreck part, but the other wanted to run fast and far.

It clung to my curves, leaving little for the imagination. I clenched my sweaty palms, let out a deep breath and opened the door to see him sitting on the bed in boxers. An unmistakable bulge tenting them.

Run! Run! My legs were frozen in place. The bulge making a ninety-degree angle sticking straight out as he stood. Noting my eyes pasted to the object of my fear, he sat.

"I'm sorry. It happens. You're so beautiful and... You should be happy it works..." Nervous garble escaped his mouth.

Like a statue, I stood in that spot, swallowing my fear. The dildo was smaller and Greta was so gentle. *Would he be gentle? Careful? Would it hurt? Would it pinch, but much more?*

"I can't take my eyes off you and it's not going to go away until I stop thinking about how beautiful you look," he said as he stepped towards me. "I understand. It's my first time too." He grabbed my hands. "But I want this, I want you." Standing so close, the bulge rubbed against my leg, he continued, "You want to see it. Look." He let my hands go and pulled his boxers down. "See, it's natural. It happens because it has to so we can..."

He kissed my neck, my chest, cupped my breasts and wiggled my nipples. "You're so perfect," he whispered in my ears.

I closed my eyes and imagined Greta, put myself in the north wing with her as we explored and pleasured each other. His lips met mine, his tongue slipping through my parted lips. My mind pretending he was Greta, ignoring the sound of his voice, I kissed him back, attempted to give him the passion I gave her.

We walked backwards until we dropped onto the bed, me on top. My legs straddling him and that darn bulge hard between my legs. A sensation of pleasure twinged as he rubbed it against me. Maybe it wouldn't be so bad.

He continued kissing me, fondling my hills and valleys and private regions. I built up my courage and touched the bulge. It was much softer than I thought, like velvet. It leaked and warm liquid dribbled over my hand. I pulled it back. "I don't think I can wait much longer. I need you, Debbie," he whispered in my ear as he rolled me over and pulled a thin, balloon-like object out of a foil package. I knew what it was -- a condom. I heard the girls at school talk about them.

He rolled it over his distended, enlarged penis then brought his arms over me and undid the snaps on the bottom of the negligee. He slid it up my hips and brought himself over me. His bulge pushing between my legs. "Are you ready?" he asked in a husky voice.

I nodded. I hadn't expected the bulge pressed against me to feel so good but it was touching and rubbing a very sensitive area. He tried pushing it in but my body seemed to reject it as it wouldn't fit. That didn't stop him as he moved his hand between my legs and guided it inside me.

My body went through a variety of feelings and emotions. At times it felt good, and when I closed my eyes I put myself in the north wing with Greta and pretended she was using the dildo on me, but when I opened them and saw his face, serious, concentrated, I remembered where I was and what I was doing. I think the worst part was feeling that I was cheating on Greta, betraying her in some way.

It didn't take him more than a couple minutes once he was all the way in, before his mouth opened wide, releasing a growl, as his body shuddered and dropped onto me then he rolled onto his back.

"That was... incredible," he said between breaths. "I could... do... that every day."

He propped his head onto an arm and traced my cleavage and stomach. "We should try again. I promise I'll last longer. The first time is like that. I couldn't hold it. It just felt so amazing!" he carried on, my eyes wandered towards his bulge that wasn't quite as large as it had been but something was wrong, missing.

"The condom!" I shouted, sitting upright and climbing off the bed. I tossed the sheets.

He looked at himself, "Oh shit!" and jumped off the bed, after stripping it of covers, sheets, and pillows he gawked at me.

"Where is it?" I asked in desperation.

He swallowed and stared at my nakedness, his eyes exploring my body until they reached my private area. "There's only one place left."

Completely horrified, I shouted at him, "Well get it out!"

With care, he put his finger inside me, small tingles jilted me and he pulled something out, hanging on the tip of his finger was the condom. The swelling emotions in me rose to the surface and I laughed so hard I doubled over.

He caught me around the middle and tossed me backwards against the pillows. "I want to marry you when I graduate in four years. I want you to be my wife."

My laughter simmered as I contemplated his words. At sixteen, I'd never thought seriously about marriage, figured it would happen one day so instead of an actual answer I shut him up with a kiss. He managed, between breaths, to ask for a second round, a do-over to get it right.

The experience wasn't horrible as much as it wasn't great but maybe over time it would get better. He'd improve

and not only meeting his testosterone-
driven needs but mine too.

Full Circle

It was two days before my grandmother's will reading when one of my death visions came true. I was powerless to stop it.

It was a clear day, a few puffy, swirling clouds but warm, no rain, and, unusually, not muggy.

Mother Nature blessed us with perfection as happened a few days each year. Maybe if I'd understood Mother Nature's warning signs, I'd have understood but, as life had it, I was an emotional train wreck of a teenager on a deep, downward spiral.

That night as we slept, Mother Nature changed her mind. The beauty of the day destroyed by the savage night. "Girls, up, down to the cafeteria now," called Ms. Johnson as she opened our door. She quickly moved onto the others. Footsteps, grumbling, and tired girls rushed into the hallway but even they weren't louder than what was brewing outside.

Winds and rain beat against the solid old house so loud it sounded like it was inside the room. We followed the crowd of confused, scared girls into the hallway as the teachers shepherded us into the only room in the entire house without windows.

We were coming up on the west wing when glass shattered. The sound rang on my mind as I suddenly flashed back to the vision I'd had two years previous. The flashback was mottled with a familiar feeling, an itch that said I'd been here before. The situation wasn't new. It was more than the fact that I'd already seen everything play out. There was something unusually, extra sinister about the winds and torrential rains. When my brain sifted through the fuzz of memories to the present event I remembered a girl was trapped by a tree as it broke through a heavy glass window.

Panic gripped me, twisted through my body in a wave of anxiety. Frantically, I searched for Robin, Lissa, and Greta, groping through the darkness and wading through the other girls. I was too late. In a surreal moment my vision and reality collided as a large branch the size of a tree trunk plunged through the window and into a girl, pinning her to the wall.

Even before I saw her face, my guts twisted and my brain exploded --

Lissa. Panic and screaming filtered into my ears as I dropped to the floor and crawled towards her. "Lissa!" I shrieked. The call never leaving my vocal cords but stuck somewhere between my brain and throat.

If I could just move the branch, unpin her, she'd be fine. "Lissa, Lissa," I called, feet and girls stepping around me, rushing past me.

I touched her foot and crawled up the wall. "Lissa, don't worry." She didn't respond, her head hung limp and awkward to the side. I put my hands under the log to heft it out of the way. My brain scrambled and not thinking clearly.

When I touched the log, sticky syrup stuck to my hands. The branch was too heavy. When I pulled my hands away they were covered in a thick, viscous, red fluid. My brain having a delayed reaction screamed as I pressed my hands to her face. "Lissa, Lissa."

A hand on my shoulder and one around my waist pulled me away through the halls and down the stairs. Tears flowing from my eyes like a tub faucet turned to full blast.

Ms. Timble and Ms. Johnson set me down. Ms. Johnson saying something I didn't understand. Ms. Timble closed the heavy doors behind us. It was all a blur after that until morning. At some point, I think I slept out of pure exhaustion.

My body and mind flat, we wandered outside. The sun again shining on us, clouds swirling in the sky.

Ella Louise's wedding dress clung to the tops of two large white oaks. I thought of Greta wearing it and our fake wedding. So many memories were tied to it.

An arm wrapped around my middle. Without looking, I folded myself into that person. Her familiar scent caught my nose, even stuffy my nose recognized the smell -- Greta.

Lissa died the minute that thick, old branch was hurled through the window by maddening winds. It was the sharp small branch attached to it that punctured an artery and she bled out in the west wing.

The hurricane was so small in width it followed a direct path to the school as a category 4. Soon after it left us and, by morning, it was downgraded to a tropical storm.

Why Lissa? People around me always dying, seeing their deaths. *Why?* Why see them if I could do nothing to stop them?! I hated the stupid *touch* I was touched with. I wanted nothing to do with it. *Leave me alone!* I screamed inside my head. She was a good person, smart, talkative, never shy or afraid to speak her mind.

The damage done to the school was so extensive the school closed for rebuilding. All the girls went home. I didn't have a home to return to, or at least not one I wanted to return to.

The mausoleum wasn't touched so I grabbed all the money my grandmother had sent over the past few years. A sigh escaped my lips as I caught sight of all the journals and logs I'd brought here, glad I had or they'd be spread over the grounds now and probably half of Louisiana.

A little over two thousand dollars I counted. I'd make it last as long as I could then I'd find something else, a way to make money. I stayed off the main road leading to the school and went through the woods until I neared New Orleans and found my way to the bus station. I bought a one-way ticket to Baton Rouge and Gabriel at Louisiana State University.

My mind resting and thinking unclearly as I leaned against the backrest, tears swelled in my eyes. Movement and thought kept the events of the last twenty-four hours from taking hold but now they flooded forward. I couldn't go home to my aunt. Ella Louise School was out of commission for an unknown amount of time. If I called Miss. Dresdan she'd have no option but to call my aunt. Gabriel was my only option. It was he who said he wanted to marry me and it couldn't be so bad. He always treated me right, even waited for me to be his first.

What I didn't expect when I arrived was how difficult it would be to find his dorm. After careful searching, I found his room, unlocked and empty. My body worn down and exhausted from the mental and physical strain, I dropped onto his bed, exhausted.

It was the next evening I woke up to fingers stroking my face, moving down my chin. When I opened my eyes Gabriel smiled at me. "What are you doing here?" his voice filled with surprise.

"The school it… it's gone." I couldn't stop the tears from welling in my eyes.

He kissed my cheek and whispered, "I'm glad you weren't injured or worse like the girl who…"

His voice drifted off as the familiar warmth of tears welled in my eyes. Through sniffles I said, "I don't have anywhere to go."

His hands traced down my sides and hips then over as they crawled between my legs. I pushed him away. "I thought you'd understand."

His face close to mine, warm, minty breath tickled my cheeks. "I do."

No, he didn't, but what were my options? His hands groping me and his mouth working its way around my face and neck. *What choice did I have? Could I push him away, deny him?* The last thing I wanted was sex with him or anyone. I wanted him to take me in his arms and tell me everything would be OK. "Gabriel I don't think now is the time," I mouthed, nearly inaudible.

His hands fumbling with a condom, he slid his pants down, exposing his firm bulge, and rolled it over until it was firmly in place and completely covered then pushed my pants and underwear down, guiding himself inside me. His breathing heavy, his mind on one thing, he didn't hear my sniffles or notice my clenched fists as he moved in and out of me, driving deeper and harder with each thrust until he stopped and I felt it shrivel inside me.

When he finished his eyes filled with despair, his fingers lightly wiping the tears on my cheeks. "I thought you wanted it too, enjoyed it. What's wrong?"

I swallowed back my sniffles long enough to say, "I'm scared and all you want is sex." I rolled over, smashing my face into the pillow.

"I'm so sorry. You do this to me, turn me into someone I'm not. Really, it's not me. I desire you. I can't help it. Don't be scared, things work out, they always do." His fingers raked through my hair, pushing loose strands behind my ears.

He folded his arms around me and lifted me upward and onto his lap and held me as I wept in his arms. My skin smashed against that bulge of his, formed again, making me cringe.

Noticing it himself, he laid me back on the bed and pulled his legs over the side. "I'm going to get us some food. Please get dressed while I'm gone."

Over pizza, we talked and he agreed to let me stay but I had to stay out of sight since it was a single room and against college dorm policy for him to harbor someone in the room. After the first couple weeks I realized the only reason he agreed was so he could have sex, sometimes only once a day but usually two times or more, between classes, after classes and on occasion I wondered if he even skipped classes. No doubt he was *Trojan's* best customer.

I hoped his sex drive would wear down but it didn't. Without any options, I wasn't sure what to do. If I stayed it was like White Oak all over again, hidden away from the world, no friends, no contact with anyone but my captor. Stockholm Syndrome came to mind. *Was that me?* I tried to remember from psychology last year what the exact definition was, but couldn't. I do know it had something to do with captives forming a bond with their captor.

The days turned into weeks, months. He was a slob, dropping his clothes on the floor, his books on the floor, occasionally on the desk but never neat. He'd clean out his pockets and lay wrinkled wads of money on the desk, dresser, floor, and shelves, sometimes even on the sink. Once I realized he'd never miss it, I collected it for myself.

Coming to stay with him was the wrong idea. I shouldn't have. Every day, several times a day, the thoughts roved my brain, but I always came to the same conclusion. *Where else would I go?* With nothing else to do I kept the room and bathroom clean. It adjoined to the next room and to stay clean myself I learned his neighbor's routine. I read his books and sometimes did his homework. Stockholm echoed again in my head. I'd grown completely dependent on him. I was his personal sex doll, maid, and servant. I depended on him for everything.

He wasn't mean, didn't yell, always greeted me with a smile. Occasionally we watched a movie on his fancy DVD player, snuggled on his bed, of course that close proximity led to another round of sex. It wasn't the worst life I'd lived but I yearned to leave, considered leaving, but always faced with where would I go. There was nowhere for me.

He came home one evening, agitated. His handsome face harrowed and hollow, hands folded behind his back he paced, after drawing the curtains completely closed. When I asked him what was wrong his lips curled into a fake smile, the edges of his lips quivering. "Nothing" was his response, followed by a fake smile. I suggested we leave, go out for dinner which we never did. Never went anywhere, at least I didn't.

"No. No." He locked the door and took me in his arms. "We'll stay here."

I turned my head when he attempted to kiss me. "Something is wrong. You might as well tell me."

He swallowed, his eyes shifting away from me, face in deep consternation. "There was an accident on campus."

"What kind of an accident?"

"The kind where someone died. The police are questioning everyone all over the campus. It's scary out there." The quiver in his voice, inability to look in my eyes, I understood then he was lying.

The next morning, still frazzled, he left the laptop he always brought to class on the desk. I'd seen him type in his password hundreds of times. I clicked the browser and it opened up to a picture of me, front news. Sixteen-year-old Debbie Chargois, granddaughter of Mrs. Holstead, heiress... fortune... if seen... reward... I read it over. *Is that why he was so jumpy?*

I did a search for any accidents at the college or in Baton Rouge related to the college but nothing came up for yesterday. There was plenty in the form of accidents, crime in the past, but nothing recent. My confirmation he was lying. *What was he thinking?* The reward was sizable, but his family was rich, he didn't need to turn me in and throw me to the wolves. *Was he afraid someone else would see me, find me, and turn me in? Or was he worried he'd lose his sex toy?*

No, if he wanted the money he would have already turned me in. However, that was the nail in the coffin. I had to go. Without wasting a moment or considering my options, because that would keep me locked in Gabriel's room, I collected my belongings and all his money I'd accumulated, slid a pair of his sunglasses over my eyes and rolled and tucked my thick wad of hair into a ball cap that did nothing but collect dust on a shelf.

I blended with the other students, no one paid any mind to me as I walked off the campus. After wandering aimlessly for a bit, quite lost, exactly the way I came in. The bus station was far easier to find and I bought a ticket to the only place I knew a person could hide indefinitely -- New Orleans.

Seduction

The two thousand dollars went quick, even though I'd found a room cheap. It wasn't in the best area but they didn't ask for ID or any questions. Across the street was a club -- Seduction. The neon lights flashed through the curtains every night. Men, hardly gentlemen, entered and exited. Young women passed through the alley with their large bags as they headed toward the back door.

Each blink of *Seduction, Girls* called to me, offered me solace in the form of cash money. It was seedy and dirty but also anonymous -- Amaryllis, the stage name I chose in a quick moment from the delicate ring Gabriel had given me. Low illumination inside the club offered cover as I danced on the stage, men throwing money at my feet. They bought me alcoholic beverages I merely sipped on to flirt with them, make them feel special.

In an awkward way, their attentions made me feel special, but also foul and confused. I flirted and laughed at their tasteless jokes, accepting twenties, hundreds, and mostly ones -- torn and weathered, not crisp.

Camille, an older dancer who'd taken a liking to me, primped my hair as I gazed into the vanity mirror, bulbs spaced around it and brightly lit. I closed my eyes as a cramp tore through me. The last couple days they'd gotten worse, stronger than the usual period ones, and today they were intermittent with nausea.

"Are you sure you're OK to dance tonight? You aren't looking so good, sweetie." She sat on the stool next to me. Her hair red as flames, her brown eyes filled with worry and concern.

I nodded, unable to speak as my insides racked with pain.

She pressed a hand on my forehead. "You're burning up. Here, take one of these." She dug into her bag and opened a little bottle then dumped two pills into her hand. "It's ibuprofen. If you're still burning up when I get back I'm taking you straight to the hospital. You hear?"

I nodded then swallowed the pills. They offered some relief for the cramps but didn't help the nausea one bit. I worked to catch my breath as the pain eased but not for long. Her words echoing in my head 'straight to the hospital, straight to the hospital'.

I couldn't go to a hospital. I just couldn't, so I pulled myself together and remembered to breathe when my vision blurred. *Hold it together, Debbie! Why, why was I in such pain?* If I could cross the street then I could lie in the bed. I had enough money for the week. I'd dance in a day or two when the cramps subsided. They never stayed. Once my period started, they'd stop.

The back door appeared a million miles away as I staggered towards it, my bag over my shoulder. A hand on the wall, I stayed close to it, used it to support me.

"Too much tonight. You'll feel better in the morning," chuckled one of the dancers. Her voice sounding like she was talking into a tube.

I didn't respond as I stepped into the alley, so dizzy I was disoriented, and it felt like forever before I got to the street. Through the thick fog in my head and the pain of each step I didn't recognize my surroundings. Another cramp bulldozed me to the ground and blackness filled my head.

When I woke I was in a hospital bed. A doctor strolled into the room, his voice sounding as if it was underwater but I was able to make out: "ectopic... methotrexate... you're lucky your friend found you... the nurse will be in to help you complete the forms."

Panic, sheer terror, my aunt. Visions of living in that house alone with her crowded my head. I remembered like it was yesterday, staying locked up in my room. My life now wasn't great but I had freedom, money. When I turned eighteen in a year I'd get a real place and a real job.

Camille walked into the room. She sat on the edge of my bed. "What were you trying to do? You hit your head on the concrete giving yourself a concussion on top of everything else going on with you."

"I can't stay here. I can't."

She whispered, "Sweetie, I know you're a runaway. I've been doing this a long time and I recognize one soon as I see one. It's easy to hide in a city of sin. I'll get you outta here, but first you need to rest. Go to sleep or pretend to be and I'll be back tomorrow."

My psychic instincts kicked in. I didn't have a vision but a feeling something dreadful was afoot. That edgy gut instinct that told me I had to make a choice, stay in the hospital until tomorrow waiting for Camille, pretend I was sleeping or suffering amnesia to avoid their questions, or sneak out.

All my belongings were in the chair and so the choice that wasn't really a choice was made. I pulled out the IV and slipped into my clothes. My head still a bit unclear but the pain in my abdomen temporarily gone anyways.

I made sure the coast was clear as I drew back the curtain and peeked my head out. A nurse passed by and I drew my head in like a turtle. After she passed I hurried to the doors, swung them open to a large waiting room filled with people. I turned my head and read the sign behind me *Emergency Room*. There was nothing between me and the big exit doors.

I had no idea what part of town I was in or how to get back to my room. I didn't even have money on me so I walked, wandered until the sun peered over the horizon. The pains came back, dull at first, but I knew I was close. The area was familiar from years ago. The museum came into view. My first field trip with the Ella Louise School for Girls.

A second wind. I was close. Cringing down the pain that came and went, I moved forward. A man opened the door to a business, grabbing my attention. He could give me directions. I ran, the bag weighing on my shoulder was starting to hurt but, like the other pain, I pushed it aside as I gingerly attempted to run. "Sir, sir."

He turned as I closed in on him. His eyes and face as familiar as the museum. The sign *Destiny's Home of Voodoo* behind his head. Her grandson. I couldn't remember his name, it'd been so many years, but I remembered he gave me a card with his phone number. Never had I called it.

He searched my face with familiarity. "Do I know you?"

I nodded. "A long time ago." I flinched in pain. "Can you give me directions?"

A warm smile took over his lips and his gentle voice spoke, "I learned from my grandmother to always tell a woman she was beautiful but you are looking very peaked, your cheeks are flush, your forehead sweaty. Come in and sit down, rest, and I'll give you directions wherever you want to go." His face pinched in concern and his words filled with unease.

My body in pain and feeling faint, I took him up on his offer and walked inside the store, following him through the wooden beads to the backroom.

"I have an apartment upstairs, let me make you something to eat. You can rest there." His words so kind and gentle and I was in no position to argue.

The apartment decorated so masculine with its beige walls, plain blue curtains, and striped sofa. He brought me a bottled water, even opened it for me.

"Egg and cheese croissant sound OK?"

I nodded and my stomach grumbled. I absorbed the small space as he cooked. A nook in the corner comprised the entire kitchen with a small, dorm-sized refrigerator, brick walls, double sinks and two-burner oven. A couple steps to my right led to a bedroom area. Like the living room, it was simple. A few paintings of the Louisiana countryside and swamp hung on the walls.

He brought me a plate, setting it on the low coffee table in front of my legs. "I have to get down to the store, but eat and feel free to nap on the couch or in the bed."

The food tasted good and the water quenched my thirst. My stomach settled, I laid my head onto the pillow resting near the arm of the couch and fell into sleep.

Unsure how long it was later, several hours at least as starlight and moonlight streamed through the window.

"Sleeping Beauty is awake."

I vaguely remembered everything. "I have to get home." I nearly jumped off the couch, the pains much duller than they'd been.

"I'll drive you, but first tell me, Debbie Chargois, what on earth are you doing wandering around New Orleans?"

I swallowed. "No need to drive me. Thank you."

"Whatever you are running from is your business. I only know who you are because your face was all over the news. Listen, I'm not contacting the authorities, obviously there's more going on and you don't have to tell me or explain anything." He stepped closer to me, his face grim. "If I wanted the reward I would have already called. Someone did turn you in." He stepped close enough he placed his hands on my arms.

"What do you want?"

He shrugged. "Nothing. Only to see you safe. If you ran it was for a reason, like I said. You aren't a small child but a nearly grown woman. If you choose, I'd like you to stay here. I can even offer you a job once you're feeling better."

I stepped back, his arms dropping to his sides. "Why are you being so nice?"

"No one's life is brimming with sunshine every day, even rich people. When I laid eyes on you this morning, you looked like death. Whatever you went through, whatever you're going through, I want to help. This voodoo shop wasn't my choice profession." He moved to the couch and sat, cupping his hands together. "I wanted to be a counselor; a therapist. Even got my degree, but when my grandmother died there was no one else to run the shop."

"You could have sold it." I stepped closer and set my bag down.

"I could have, but it's an established business and brings in more money than counseling so I made a choice thinking I'd one day hire a manager, let them run it, but I know the voodoo rituals my grandmother performed and that's what people pay good money for. I couldn't trust it in the hands of someone else."

I deliberated on his proposition. I didn't like dancing and wasn't keen on the place I was staying. If anyone turned me in it was Camilla, had to be. The doctor didn't know, he was going to send in a nurse to help me complete the paperwork. It had to be Camilla and I didn't blame her. The amount of money offered she could stop dancing and go to school to find a better career. I wasn't sure how old she was but didn't think even under the dark lights of the club her body would hold many more years. "OK, but can you take me to my room to collect my things?"

Destiny's House of Voodoo

After a few days I was feeling much better and the pains completely subsided. I used that time to search the internet for the words I heard the doctor say "ectopic" and "methotrexate". According to the website an ectopic pregnancy occurs when an egg is fertilized in the fallopian tube like normal but doesn't drop into the uterus. The embryo continues to grow but can't survive. It's fatal for the developing embryo and can be fatal to the mother if untreated. Methotrexate may be used to terminate an ectopic pregnancy as it stops the cells from dividing.

Gabriel -- it was his. Somehow, one of those many times, sperm slipped out and found their path up my cervix. The time I spent with him rushed back, not just in his dorm but throughout my teenage years. Now away from him, with no prospect of ever seeing him again, I realized how strange he and our relationship were. Even though he smiled with me it wasn't the kind of full-bodied smile Cole gave me daily. It was edged in darkness, ominous.

He never talked about his family. I knew so much about Cole's and I'd only been in his house not even a week. Gabriel took me places, spoiled me, yet I never really knew him. I'd never thought while we were together about the age difference, not that it was much, but for a junior in high school to date a girl in the eighth grade made no sense, except Landsom was an all-boys school but college was co-ed yet he had no girlfriend except me.

My life brightened each day Cole was in it. His dimples riding his smiling cheeks and his contagious laughter.

"What do you say we get out of here tonight?" he asked as his foot hit the last step.

He didn't have to ask twice. I needed normalcy, which I felt with him. I wasn't persecuted or hidden from the world or hiding my inappropriate relationship by dating a broody young man. No, I was free finally. "Can we eat near the river?"

"Anything you want."

The breezes swept over us, pushing away all the dismal reality of my life. I was caught in a moment I didn't want to end. "I see things," I confessed to him. Holding my breath, I waited for his response.

When he did answer after a few minutes he said, "My grandmother gave everyone the heebie jeebies She did it on purpose. It was part of the act. Voodoo, once a strong religion in these parts, is now a waning art. Most people are interested in the magic and spooky, commercial aspect of it."

I giggled with the memory. "She did freak us out. The dark lights and she looked so old. The shadows from the candlelight made her look so ghostly."

"She was old." He chuckled. "I was mostly raised by her. That day after you left she told me 'that high yellow girl will be back. You must take her in and care for her without asking any questions'. You see, my grandmother saw things too."

Was he saying he expected me? That old, wrinkled woman -- she always knew. I thought back to her words about digging in a well, not liking what I might find. What did she know about me?

"I didn't ask the morning I found you and I'm not asking now unless you want to share."

The calm sincerity in his voice. I put my hand on his chin and he turned his head so our eyes met. "It's a very long story."

"We have all night."

So I told him how my family died when I was a baby and how I was sent to live with my horrible family who tormented, abused, and neglected me. I was sure there were memories buried deep that I didn't remember. My grandmother's miraculous recovery and the Ella Louise School. I even told him the story about Gabriel and the ectopic pregnancy.

He brushed my windblown spirals off my face. "You want to get a drink?"

His question took me by surprise. I opened up and that's it. No judgement, no 'I'm sorry for your horrible situation'. "I'm only seventeen."

He smiled wide, showing his dimples. "It's New Orleans, drinking is a city-wide phenomena. No one will notice."

As we walked, we talked. "Sounds like you had a hard life. My life was pretty easy, but not my brother's. I barely remember him though. I only met him a couple times."

"Tell me about him."

"Not a lot to say. All I remember is him throwing me in the air and catching me. I was all smiles and laughter. We had different fathers. His was a man who killed himself when he stumbled into a ditch, drunk, and passed out. He never woke up. My mother came home after his death, went to school, became a court reporter and married a lawyer then they had me. My brother left home, met a woman and got married before he died very young." He shrugged.

"That's awful. I'm so sorry."

"We're here. Grab a seat and I'll get us beverages."

Growing Seed

Cole and I had a lot in common, we grew closer each day. I helped him out in the store and my identity stayed secret. I'd cut my hair to shoulder-length and had color put in it. I barely looked like myself. Occasionally customers gave me glances as if they recognized me but soon forgot. My face wasn't in the news any longer. The part of my life I missed was Miss. Dresdan. I wondered if she was still alive and healthy. Each day I longed to call her but reminded myself of my aunt and life at White Oak. I'd be eighteen in a matter of months then I'd be free of her forever.

The bell on the door of Destiny's Home of Voodoo rang, alerting me someone had entered the store. Parting the beaded curtains, I welcomed the customer. A middle-aged woman with blond hair so light I'd never seen anything like it. Her eyes were the most distinctive feature as they were two different colors. Her long dress flowed when she walked as if an invisible breeze were pushing it. She was ethereal and I almost wondered if she was real or my *sight* acting up.

"Welcome to Destiny's," I said with a smile.

An inviting, composed smile crossed her face and something else was attached to her giving me the notion she knew more about what she was going ask than I did. "I have a bit of a ghost problem. Do you have anything that may help me?"

"That depends on the ghost problem. We have a few items that may help but if you're looking for a ritual Cole can help you with that," I said, really hoping she and the uneasy vibe I was pulling from her would turn around and leave the store.

I stayed behind the counter, my hands resting, tented on it. She dropped a hand over mine. A mutiny of ominous, murky images took over my mind, seizing my body in terror. I couldn't move or catch my breath. From the back of my mind came a screeching *Move your hands! Move them!*

As if the customer read my mind, she took her hand off mine in a quick gesture. She leaned over the counter, one amber eye, one green eye, locked me into a gaze. "We are harbingers of death. You have to own it to make a difference." She walked away, her low heels clicking against the floor. The steady rhythm echoing in my head as she exited the store.

A few minutes, or maybe several minutes later, possibly even an hour or so, Cole came up behind me. "Debbie?"

I turned to see his handsome face riddled with concern. "You haven't moved in a few minutes. Is something wrong?"

I cleared my throat. "Not exactly. A customer kind of freaked me out is all."

He chuckled and wrapped an arm around my waist. "We get them. The weirdoes, the freaks. They flock to the Voodoo store. Most are harmless, don't let it scare you much."

He was right. She wasn't the first strange one I'd met since working at the store. She was, however, the first one that sent me visions.

Cole moved around the counter and tidied the shelves. "You ever seen a first snow?" he asked, completely changing the subject.

"No, I've never seen any snow."

He pushed upward, shock over his face. "What? You've never seen snow?!"

I sniggered at his reaction. His eyebrows lifted and eyes enlarged, mouth in an O. "Does TV count?"

He came around the counter. "My grandparents made a good living and bought this chalet, a small thing in the mountains of Tennessee, nothing but trees for miles. They figured one day they'd sell this store and retire there, but my grandfather died. I like to visit every year for the first snow."

My brows lowered in confusion. "I think it's a great idea you should go. I can mind the store."

He grabbed my hands and spun me around in the tiny space of the cramped store. "We'll close the store. I want you to come with me."

I jumped up, wrapped my arms around his neck and gave him a huge kiss on his cheek that turned into something more. Our lips and tongues met.

"I'm sorry." I pushed back, my feet falling to the ground as he was much taller than me.

Cheer filled his eyes. "No, no. How dare you apologize for showing affection?"

The first snow due to fall in early January, he closed up the shop and we packed up the car with luggage, food, and even stopped for firewood on the way. My eyes were a wonder as I took in the landscape. Never had I left Louisiana and now I saw pieces of our neighboring states; Alabama, Mississippi, and finally, Tennessee. A lot of it looked similar to Louisiana until we reached the higher elevations.

Houses grew farther apart as we headed up the mountain road, smoke rolled through the naked trees from the chimneys. He explained how fall was spectacular as well when the leaves turned red, orange, and yellow before they dropped. Spring and summer burst with colors of the new birth of flowers. He promised we'd come back for all the seasons.

The chalet wasn't any shabbier than the scenery. Rustic wood walls and a great open room downstairs. A stone wall with a fireplace opened on both sides, the kitchen and living area. Upstairs was an open loft.

"What do you think?" he asked as he stoked the fire.

"It's really beautiful. The house, the mountains." I dropped to my knees on the floor next to him.

His dimples pressed into his cheeks as he smiled, taking his hand away from the fire long enough to draw me into a hug and give me a kiss. With him was so different than Gabriel or Greta. I guessed maturity made me view things differently. I didn't think I could love a man and settled for Gabriel, but maybe love didn't work that way at all. Is was about the person, their character and heart, and not at all about what society deemed appropriate.

My grandmother told me that when she explained the story of my biological grandfather and non-biological grandfather. She and her husband had to keep their relationships hidden from the public eye because they weren't accepted. It didn't stop their hearts from loving each other and carrying on.

The fire roaring, we snuggled together on the rug in front of it. Our arms around each other, my head on his shoulder. He kissed my head which soon led to our lips meeting in a deep kiss. I pushed his shirt over his head. Our bodies soon naked, we entwined together. The heat of the fire spread over us, my body tingled in excitement with each touch, each kiss. I welcomed him into me as we made love.

I always thought of Greta that first time, hard to forget, but with Cole she didn't come to mind until after. I thought of how different each experience was. I wanted them both, but Cole was my mature self, not the confused, sad child at Ella Louise. I wished to capture that moment forever and wished my story could end there, happily ever after.

Part 3
Death is but
a Beginning

Life's Lemons

ife had another plan for me, one I didn't see coming, but if I'd listened to the dread in my gut, acknowledged the swells of anxiety, things may have turned out differently.

On the morning of my eighteenth birthday, Cole woke me with a cake. He woke up before dawn to bake it. I blew my candles -- all eighteen -- out. He closed the store and we spent the day on a steamboat cruise up the Mississippi. As romantic as it was, it also brought back memories which I shared with Cole.

"My mom, she had a secret relationship with my dad. They even had a private spot on a houseboat. I found it many years later with a friend. We were exploring. Two children messing around where we shouldn't be. Other than bits and pieces of fragmented memories, I don't know anything about my father."

"Nothing?"

"Not really. He died before I was born but I do remember some small things about the man I thought was my father. He was really just my mom's childhood friend who helped her after my father died. It was he who was murdered with the rest of my family."

"I don't remember much about mine either but you have *sight*. I can help you remember if you want."

"You'd do that for me?"

"I'd do anything for you, haven't you figured that out yet?" he asked, his voice a little hurt. His tender hands on my face.

A couple months later, I never asked about what we spoke of on the steamboat, he informed me he'd found my parents' home. I wanted to know and I didn't. The touch and knowing wasn't so important to me, he was. "Cole." I took his hands, our eyes meeting. "I've thought a lot about this. About our discussion, and I don't think I want to know. I can't change the past and the present is all that matters."

It was against my nature to turn down answers but with so much blood and death in my life I wanted an end to it not more questions.

He searched my face, his solemn as he rolled his tongue over his upper lip. "You need to know this. It's not just… about your family… or their deaths. There's more…"

His words hung in the air, stifling the room. *What did he mean?* I took in a deep breath and my body tied into knots. I didn't respond.

A tear balanced itself on the corner of his eye, he swallowed. "I've searched and fought this, thinking it can't be correct – two people with the same name, the wrong address… Your father is a…" he stumbled over his words.

What? What was my father? Who was he? Did he do something bad to my family? Is this the tragic experience my mind needed to see to gain control of my sight? I swallowed in apprehension as the horrific words jumped off his tongue.

"My half-brother." His eyes dropped to the floor.

My mind processed his words. My father was his half-brother making him… Oh shit! Making him my half-uncle! I jumped up! "No, no! It can't be."

He shook his head as sobs wracked his body, his shoulders rising and falling in response.

"We didn't know, couldn't have known – two ships in the night. I have to leave. I can't stay!" I rushed into the bedroom and shoved clothes willy nilly into a suitcase. There was possibly one other explanation and it was time to find out.

Cole sat on the couch, his head leaned over the back, his eyes empty of their usual vibrance. I wanted to hold him, make everything OK. I couldn't, there was no OK. We slept with each other, blood relations. The thought made me shudder. Louisiana was a big enough state I'd never have guessed our families ever would have crossed paths, but secrets lurked in everyone's past. Skeletons in the cupboard, ghosts in the attic, whispering truths no one can hear.

The bus ride was long, giving my mind time to process stories from my grandmother and Miss. Dresdan. Was there any truth in them or were they ramblings from mothers distraught over their dead children, seeking solace? Arvid's coin in my hand, I rolled it between my palm and fingers as if it would show me answers instead of Arvid's childhood memories.

Guilt riddled me for leaving Cole in such a state but I couldn't, we couldn't, carry on. Not without knowing.

I sucked in a deep breath of muggy Florida air as I stepped off the bus…

Boy Trouble

The walk from the bus station helped ease my cacophony of thoughts and apprehensions. The liquid air dripped around me, moistening my shorts, tank top, and making my feet slip on the rubbery bottom of my flip-flops.

The development had a large waterfall surrounded by well-maintained double- and triple-wide trailers. It was a suburban trailer park. I chuckled at the thought. A sign welcomed me to Ashton Estates Retirement Community. Below it read Bingo Tuesdays and Thursdays, Beading Blast Saturday Morning, Yoga, swimming and gardening activities throughout the week and a Saturday night mixer. Dates, times, and locations were beside each activity.

I stopped short of a small double-wide, larger than her bungalow at White Oak. Manicured, showy flowers and coarse grass surrounded the driveway. The roof formed a small awning over the dark green front door. I lifted the knocker and let it go. A pitter patter of light steps moved towards me and the door opened, light streaming over me, breaking through the darkness from the fallen sun.

A loose gown covering her body, eyes wide in surprise. "Get in here, child. What are you doing? You in some kind of trouble?"

Her arms wide, welcoming, as I dropped my head onto her shoulder in the doorway. Gentle arms wrapped tight around me.

How did she know I was in trouble? Instinct? Did she also have the *touch?*

"Let's not linger in the doorway, come, I'll make us some tea and we can talk." She guided me to a tan couch filled with crocheted pillows of all colors. Her home was vibrant, a stark difference from her bungalow at White Oak. It was far more modern, with a sliding glass door and a large TV fastened to the wall.

Pictures of Arvid, my mother, and my brothers were in small frames on a table beside the couch. In larger frames, similar pictures hung from the walls and a few hand-painted landscapes of the bayou. Even though they captured the tall grasses and placid water they carried a cheerfulness that I didn't remember or never felt all the years I lived there.

"Boy trouble?" she enquired as she handed me a glass of sweet tea.

"Yes." I read her thoughts as her eyes drifted over my belly. "Not that kind. I'm not pregnant."

"What is it then, dear?" Her face awash with concern.

I didn't know where to start. I hadn't seen her in years, hadn't made an attempt, and now I had a huge favor to ask.

"Sit, catch your breath. When you're ready." She took a seat across from me on a matching tan chair. "We have a lot to catch up on, so I'll start." She cleared her throat. "You missed the will reading. You see, your grandmother left you as the sole heir to your family's fortune. You, Debbie, are a very rich young lady and White Oak is completely yours, but to claim it you must contact her lawyer in Baton Rouge and sign the paperwork."

What? What about my aunt, Malery?

When I didn't respond, she smiled. "It's a lot to take in, I know, and you can think about it, maybe sleep would help you out. I have extra sheets and a pillow." She set her sweet tea down on the coffee table and rose from the chair.

I leaned forward and touched her gown. "No, stay. We can talk about that later. I have something else more pressing. I met a man. He's good to me, real good. Saved me from a life that was taking me down the wrong path but…" I searched for the right words.

"That's good news, dear." She sat on the couch beside me.

"It was. It was perfect." I paused, and she held in anticipation. "You said Arvid went to my mother after my father died. How many months before I was born?"

"Oh." She leaned back. "Well, several I reckon. I don't really recall. Why do you ask such a question?"

I hesitated. "Is it possible he was my father?"

She smiled sweetly. "We've been through this. Your mother loved your father. She loved Arvid too, but not in the same way, at least not until…" Her eyes widened and the wrinkles on her forehead moved upwards as surprise lit up her face. "Oh, oh."

I nodded. "I need to know. If there's any chance you are my grandmother and Arvid was my father, I have to know."

"Oh darlin', I don't know how I missed it all these years. Your mother, when I came to visit after you were born, handed you to me and said 'say hello to your granddaughter'." She placed her hands over her mouth then dropped them. "I thought she said that because she was like a daughter to me."

"I think maybe you are my grandmother but the only way to know is a DNA test. There's a place here, close by, that does them. We can get our results in a few days."

Tears streamed her cheeks. "Love is all kinds of strange. I thought I loved Arvid's dad, but I didn't. We were young. It wasn't love, not true love. Not the kind of love that lasts a lifetime. Alma loved Arvid very much and it isn't a stretch that she finally saw him as more than a friend. We should do this testing tomorrow, first thing."

The next day we woke, ate, and drove to the clinic. Within three days we had our answer.

The Coast

The retirement community had their own private piece of beach. I'd never seen any beach or the ocean other than pictures. We took our results and walked to her favorite spot. The white sands beneath our feet and the blue-green Gulf Coast in front of us. Water splashed over our toes as we strolled.

We shared twenty-six percent the same DNA making her my paternal grandmother. It was too late to wonder how my life would have changed if she'd raised me. The past was the past repeated as an echo. She always took care of me, made me feel special, human. That day was our day but I had to get back, tell Cole.

We could still be together. He wasn't my half-uncle but my brothers'. I felt I was shortchanging her, robbing her of time for us when I left the following day. I promised her I'd be back and I'd stay for a while. Cole, though, was my priority at the moment. The look on his face when I left, he needed to know the news and I couldn't wait to tell him.

I boarded the bus, armed with my copy of our results. When I got home, he wasn't there. On the table was a note in case I returned while he was gone. He closed the shop and took a few days, heading to the cabin. I picked up the phone and called the number but there was no response. The phone rang several times.

I tried again, thinking he was out for a hike, chopping wood, or whatever he went there to do, but still no answer. Unable to wait and becoming worried, I boarded another bus and headed to Tennessee. I took the most direct path I could, only changing buses once and caught a ride up the mountain.

The door was locked so I pulled the key from under the planter. "Cole," I called, running through the cabin, up the stairs, but all I heard in return was silence. In the kitchen, dishes filled the sink. On the table, a half-drunk cup of coffee.

I nearly jumped out of my skin when someone knocked on the door and it creaked open. "Cole." I turned. A mess of curly, dark hair peppered with gray stood in the doorway. A thick beard and scruffy mustache covered his face. His head shiny bald.

"You Debbie?" he inquired; his voice as gruff as his appearance.

"Yes." The words meek as if they knew whatever he had to say was bad.

He swished his lips. "Cole's not here but I can take you to him."

I knew better than to get into cars or trucks with strangers. This man, though, didn't seem a stranger as he knew my name and Cole's. "Are you a neighbor?"

He ran a hand over his unruly hair. "I've known Cole and his family for years. We live a piece up the road." He pointed.

I nodded and joined him as we walked towards a late model blue truck. Rust ate at the bottom, along the wheel wells, and the outside of the bed. He opened the door for me and I climbed onto the passenger side of the blue, white, and gold striped cloth seat.

"I don't much enjoy bein' the bearer of this kind of news," the man said.

My heart clutched tighter than a fist at his words. No conversation started with his words ever was good.

"Cole, he was was bit by a rattler. By the time I found him he was in a bad way." The man smoothed his beard with one hand, the other on the steering wheel. "It was too late. The landline wasn't working and cell reception, um, well it works when it wants around here. He uh… got in his car and headed into town but lost control of his car trying to avoid a deer." Sorrow slipped into his gruff voice.

"What are you saying?! What?" My voice frantic, fear climbing up my bones.

He stopped tugging at his beard. "He's in the hospital, too many internal injuries, and the venom seeped into him before I found him. Truth is, I think he's waiting for you."

Waiting? What did he mean, he's waiting for me? "He's doesn't know I'm coming, why would he be waiting?" Reality hadn't sunk in. My mind refused to grasp the man's words.

"I don't think your hearin' straight. Honey, he's dying. Somehow, though, he knew you'd be comin'."

I swallowed as his words filtered through my consciousness. *Dying, he's dying.* A flood of tears threatened my eyes, I blinked to keep them at bay. No, not Cole. He'd get better, had to. I'd lost too many people in my life. Those I loved, those I hated, but too many.

The salty, telltale sign of tears welled in my throat when I laid eyes on Cole. I ran to his bedside, squatted, and took his hand. His face level with mine. A smile forced its way over his face, slow, as if it hurt for him to move, and his eyes shifted to the side, meeting mine.

In the bed he appeared so much smaller, weaker, thinner, his skin pale. "Cole, I have the best news," I managed through the tears that threatened to break free. "We aren't related. I have the proof. We can be together."

His smile didn't wane as he struggled to speak. "That's g---ood n… news. I l… love y—ou, Debbie Chargois." As if those words sucked every last bit of energy out of him, his head bobbed to the side and his hand in mine grew limp.

The tears I held at bay sprang forth with a vengeance as I draped myself over his body.

Harbingers of Death

After Cole's funeral I took his research, including our family ties, and decided it was time to fight my inner demons. The monsters that showed me death and betrayal. It was time to show the grim reaper who I was and slam the door in his face.

The blond lady with the two different colored eyes, she'd said, 'We are harbingers of death. You have to own it to make a difference.' That strange message that freaked me rested atop my brain, her words resonated inside me. Like me, she had some type of *touch* and in her way was helping me, warning me.

Johnie too, she came to terms with whatever cruelty was bestowed by her father, reliving it, and gained control of her *touch*. It was my time to halt the fatality train from taking everyone in my life.

The house of Marcus and Alma Chargois, with its creamy stucco, looked like any suburban home but I imagined all the neighborhood children told spooky stories about. Any damage the storm did to the house was repaired years ago. My grandmother made sure of that. She even tried to sell it, but no one wanted a house with three gruesome deaths attached.

The architecture of the house had varying levels, making the house appear large. I turned the key, closed my eyes, and pushed the front door open. When I opened my eyes, I was staring at an empty house. Tile floors, warm harvest-orange walls, and crown molding gave the home a cozy feel.

It didn't feel like anywhere I'd ever been. I took a step over the threshold. To my right was a kitchen. White Shaker cabinets gave it an open feel. Light streamed through the window above the double sink and a wide bar combined the kitchen and living room spaces.

Through the living room to the right, behind the kitchen, was a large bedroom, vacant of any items that might remind me of my parents. Through an alcove was a sizable walk-in closet, across from it a bathroom with a shower and tub. I ran my finger along the tub, attempting to see my mother. To remember something about her, but I came up blank.

The left side of the living room there were two bedrooms, each equal in size. One had a walk-in closet about half the size of the master. The other had built-in shelves. They weren't new. Toys, I remembered toys on them; puzzles, Legos, and little toy cars. This had been my brothers' room.

I sat on the floor of what imagined was my own room and prepped Marva's candle. I laid on the tile floor, firm against my back, and clutched my necklace. Breathing in the aroma of the candle, something didn't feel quite right.

My eyes scanned the room and kept going back to the wall opposite the closet. Light from the falling sun drifted across the room and something in the baseboard twinkled. I crawled towards it and felt along the wall until a tiny object poked my finger. Sure it was a nail or staple, I picked it up anyways. Between my fingers was a gold dragonfly earring.

I remembered it! My mother, she wore them a lot. Somehow this tiny object survived the contractors and workers who put the house back together. I knew that much. My family died during a hurricane, not because of the storm but because someone murdered them.

Lying back on the floor, I clasped my mother's earring in my hand and Arvid's coin Miss. Dresdan gave me long ago in the other, closed my eyes and breathed in the candle's fragrant scent.

I saw my brothers, both with short, dark hair, one a couple years older than the other, they ran through the house, chasing each other, building with blocks, roughhousing with their father as my mother jokingly scolded them. He was a good man and they loved him incredibly. I saw it in their faces and laughter. A happy family I was never part of.

My mother standing in the doorway, folding her hands over her face, tears, rivers of tears, as the policeman lowered his hat and walked away, leaving her a broken mess. A man's hand on my mother's thigh. Wind, loud howling wind. Arvid pounding boards over the windows.

My hands, small and pudgy, as I stuff a thumb into my mouth and hold a teddy bear. Footsteps moving closer, but the room is dark. A candle flicker frames the silhouette of a man, short, thick, with a square jaw and something in his hand that he held against his pants. It was shiny.

A scream jolted me out of slumber. I pulled myself up using the rungs on my crib. It was dark. I couldn't see anything. Outside it was loud like the hurricane at Ella Louise. Heavy footfalls moved closer, but they were muffled. The floor, it hadn't been tile but carpet. I cried and a voice spoke to me through the darkness.

A hand touched my shoulder, not warm and inviting, but cold, plasticky, like it was fake skin or… or a glove. Sending shivers coursing through my little body. "Daisy, why did your parents name you after a flower?" Disdain in the man's voice.

Then he did the most unusual thing: he sang. "All the clouds are clearin', And I think we're over the storm, Well I been pickin' it up around me, Daisy, I think I'm sane." His tone calm, gentle. It was a ballad, maybe something from the 70s by the tune of it. I sat up, wheezing, my breath caught in my throat. I remembered! That man, he murdered my family. I never saw, as I was a baby in my crib, but I remembered him. While he sang, he picked me up. His face square, jaw tight, head bald, and eyes cloudy blue. I was crying and he calmed me, laid me back in my crib, pulled a blanket up to my chin and took my teddy bear.

"One day we'll meet again. Sweet dreams, Daisy." That was it, he left. I fell asleep and when I woke there was a commotion in my house and a woman with short, dark hair picked me up. She smelled like peppermint.

My family loved each other, really loved each other. I wished more than ever I grew up in that world. Hated that man for taking them. Wanted him dead! I was no longer a child and with the financial resources my grandmother left me I would find my family's killer. Vengeance was mine!

There was one question my memories raised up: Why did he call me Daisy?

Taking What's Mine

I barged into Mr. Alexander's office. A lady with sandy blond hair sat at a desk. She pulled her dainty, gold-rimmed glasses off. "Do you have an appointment?"

"No, I'm Debbie Chargois. I believe Mr. Alexander has been searching for me for some years now," I said, taking in the shock in her green eyes.

She punched buttons on the phone with her long, red nails. "There's a Miss Chargois here to see you… yes." She eyed me then dropped the phone. "He'll be out soon."

On my long trip from Pensacola to Baton Rouge I did an internet search using the words I remembered from the song the man sang to me – Daisy Jane by America. I listened to it a few times on the trip. Its words repeating in my head.

A few black and white pictures hung on the white wall, of buildings and scenery. I assumed pictures of Baton Rouge many years past. Some included pedestrians and cars, others structures with large signs advertising the name of their business.

A door opened and a man with gold hair trimmed short and square-rimmed glasses walked towards me. I remembered his face. Mr. Alexander. His green eyes not as solemn and his face still pleasing to the eye. He extended a hand. "Miss. Chargois, nice to finally see you again. I assume you are here to claim your inheritance finally. You have been a difficult woman to track down," he drawled in a southern business-like accent. The same as I remembered.

I stood, ignoring his hand. "I am." I followed him into his office and took a seat in a leather chair he pointed me towards.

'First, there are questions I have that I believe you can answer." I pressed my hands nervously along the sides of my skirt.

"I can try." He smiled.

"Did my grandmother change my name?"

He tented his hands on the bulky, mahogany desk. "She did, for your own protection. You know what happened to your family?"

I nodded.

He continued, his voice taking on the solemn tone I remember, "She thought with a different name whoever murdered your family wouldn't come searching for you. That was always her fear."

His statement was profound. She hid me away in the bayou, locked me in the attic after Uncle's death. She claimed it was to protect me. She was scared of the ghosts and haunts of my past. "Before you ask, my name was Daisy, my grandmother was Ms. Holstead and my mother was Alma Chargois."

He stared at me oddly. "I remember you. I'm not that old." He chuckled, his tone going back to his business-like southern drawl. "I do have to request you complete a DNA test but that is standard procedure."

"Did they ever find the person who killed my family?" I asked, my words shaky.

He eyes studied a spot on the wall then shifted, meeting mine. "They believe they did but can only tie the man to one eyewitness account. A murder, matching that of your family three years prior, and the witness, well, was very young."

He pulled open a drawer and brought out a file, laying it on the desk.

Pushing it toward me he said, "It's in there."

Apprehensively, I placed my hand on the file and pulled. His fingers still on the opposite edge.

"He was murdered recently, found in a motel room with his throat slit in the same fashion as his victims. His mystery is unsolved and may remain so. Seems there was no evidence at the scene of the crime and no witnesses, or at least none that want to come forward. Karma often returns to those who do wrong." He lifted his fingers from the file.

I felt anger and relief. I was happy the man was dead but disappointed it wasn't by my own hands. I opened the file. His face stared at me under the headlines. The same man who sang Daisy Jane to me and laid me in bed. He robbed me of a life filled with good memories and love. Instead I was abused, neglected, treated like less than a person.

Anger and rage ignited a fire in me. I had other scores that could be settled. I pushed the file back towards him and stood. "How is my aunt?"

He pushed his chair back and stood. "Mrs. Gipher will set everything up for you." Mr. Alexander walked around his chair. "I'll see you out."

As we strolled outside, he talked. "Your aunt, Miss. Chargois, killed herself soon after your grandmother's death. The maid found her in the bathtub with an empty bottle of sleeping pills. It was too late, she was gone."

The last time I saw my aunt I saw the bathtub overflowing with bloody water, a hand over the side. I didn't look too close but all I needed was to look at the hand. Skinny fingers and wrinkles webbed over the surface. My aunt's. I'd seen her death too. Fate had ousted me again. No remorse flowed through my veins, only more rage that I didn't get the opportunity to do it myself. "Thank you, Mr. Alexander."

I spent the night in Baton Rouge while I waited again for DNA results. I had nowhere else to go anyways and Grandma's money paid for the fancy hotel Mr. Alexander put me up in. Unable to sleep, with an uneasy feeling creeping in my gut, I went for a walk, stopping to watch the waters of the Mississippi as the sun set on the horizon.

Color spread over the surface creating an orangey-pink glow in the center until only the lights of the city danced on top. Cars whizzed by me as I strolled the city. It was so different than New Orleans. Not as free-spirited and artistic, more conservative. Yet, there were similarities, old buildings – echoes of the past.

"Debbie," someone called, drawing me out of my thoughts. I paused for a moment. The voice called again, "Debbie." I turned around to see who was addressing me. A man stood on the other side of the street, tall, dark hair. Our eyes locked – Gabriel.

I didn't have time to think or react before he took a step into the street, right in front of a moving car. The grille striking his body made the worst thud before he hit the ground. "Help, someone call 911," the driver screamed as he flew to the front of the car.

The grim reaper's hand maiden, another vision fulfilled. Nothing stopped, death followed me. The first time Gabriel kissed me, the moments we spent together while I was at Ella Louise flashed in my head followed by the bad memories. How I was his sex slave.

I'd run two blocks before I realized it and stopped. I wasn't going back. A couple, holding hands, strolled by me, their eyes glowered at me, even as they passed. Not watching where they were going. Suddenly the couple was laughing and joking, their eyes on each other. *Was I seeing things?*

Voices in the Attic

My parents' deaths were only half of the darkness surrounding me. The other half, a hell created by my family. The doors to the devil's play yard opened into the great room of White Oak Plantation.

Weathered pillars holding the veranda stood against the cracked and peeling paint. It was a mere skeleton of the great house it was back in the 1700s when it was built. I entered, a musty, mildewy smell drifted through my nostrils and dust swirled around me. The particles visible in the soft, blurry light from the windows.

Creaks and moans followed me up the steps. I paused by my room and glanced inside. The crimson bedspread standing out against the white walls. Silence deafened my ears as I continued down the hall and up the steps, stopping in front of the attic door. Sadness and neglect overwhelmed me as I drew in a long breath and pushed the door open. I clutched the locket around my neck. I knew, had known for some time, it wasn't my mother's. That was a childhood fantasy. It belonged to some other ancestor. She guided me to finding things in the house, the distillery wasn't what I was meant to find but I was a child and not in control of my *touch*. I didn't understand.

Light filtered through the window, blanketing the room in soft light. I pushed the cypress chest out of the way and unlocked the door. The room appeared empty except for the other chest. "Where? Show me," I whispered, raising the locket over my head and resting it in the palm of my hand.

The image of a woman, prying up a floorboard, flooded my vision. I went to the spot and stepped along the boards searching for the loose one. I pried it up and inside was a tattered leather journal. The first page read:

February 11, 1793

My womb is but a coffin. It cannot bear a child and I cannot bear to lose another...

On my bed I read every entry in the diary of my great, great, great, great, great grandmother. She and my grandfather: the builders of White Oak. In ten years of marriage she lost six babies to miscarriages and a seventh was stillborn. She allowed her husband to take on a concubine, a high-yellow slave girl. They brought her into the house. Set her up in my room, my mom's room -- the third on the right. It was as if her spirit had been speaking to me all these years, begging me to learn the truth. To free her of the shackles of White Oak.

The words on paper turned into a vision in my head as I read. She became pregnant and my grandmother pretended to be pregnant at social gatherings. She went into labor. A black midwife brought in, sweat pouring off the slave girl's face as she pushed her son out into the world. He was white as new fallen snow with black hair that stood up on top like a Hershey's Kiss. His cheeks chubby and reddened from the strain of birth. A loud wail shook his little body as the midwife cleaned and wrapped him in a tiny blanket and handed him to my grandmother.

They sold the slave girl after that to a nearby plantation, for a cheap price being as she was a "problem", to a man who was known for reforming slaves. I could only imagine that meant nothing but agony. She never even got to see her baby grow up. She never even held him, not once. They took the child and raised him as their own.

My grandmother, who hand-pumped her breastmilk for months, fed him from her own tit. She'd planned the whole thing after losing their last baby.

The slave girl, her high cheek bones, heart-shaped chin, and long, dark hair looked much like my grandmother in her youth. She was striking. Over the next few months her eyes became hollow holes and tears of pain spilled over cheeks, cascading onto my own as they dropped onto the pages of the diary.

Like a heart-wrenching stab in my chest I was unable to put the diary down. When she couldn't bear it anymore, she ran away, straight to White Oak during a thunderstorm to retrieve her baby boy or die. She was aware of the consequences. She didn't reach the front door before she was caught and dragged back, literally – hog-tied at her hands and feet -- through the mud and standing water. Her small, frail shell of a once-vibrant body twisted in the mud that forced its way up her nose and down her throat every breath she took until she didn't take anymore.

They tossed her dead body, still hog-tied, into the bayou where they pushed it down. Torrents of rain washing over their faces as they treated her like a piece of trash. There was no concern or remorse for her life. She was a "runaway" slave. That's what they called her. The truth buried deep in the waters.

November 13, 1816

My guilt has eaten away at me for all these years but the truth can never be told. My son would lose everything because a slave cannot own property. They are property and if it was ever learned what we did, White Oak would be sold to the next white person in line and he would be sold as a slave.

It is our love for him that keeps this secret. His wife, Margery, is pregnant with their first child but I may not live to see him as my lungs are weak and my body a shell.

I hope one day my grandchildren will live in a world that doesn't see color, where slavery doesn't exist. It is my son who taught me true love and acceptance.

I beg God for his forgiveness, even though I do not deserve it.

It's Time

I gathered together an item from everyone involved. I never really believed my grandmother's explanation. In my heart, I knew it at the time, even though my overactive brain saw what she wanted me to. That my uncle watched me with a lustful eye but, when I thought back, I didn't truly remember him ever paying much mind to me. I was a ghost to him, even in the same room he never glanced my way and he worked everyday almost, even when the bridges got flooded from rain. Somehow he found a way to escape this place daily.

My aunt and uncle's wedding rings, my grandma's vanity mirror, my father's letters to my mom, my mom's earring, and even the coin Miss. Dresdan gave me of her son's, I laid out in a circle on the floor. He was a best friend to my mom and the man who raised me until his unfortunate death. The candle still lit and its sweet, spicy scent permeating the entire room, I placed my hands over the items, drawing in their energy, and inhaled deeply, allowing the spirits' voices inside my head. The haunts and whispers of the past flashed over my mind.

Fractured images appeared. My aunt handing money to a man in a cowboy hat and boots. His face not visible. Miss. Dresdan's son watching the transaction, racing down the bayou road, his car breaking down, steam pouring from the radiator. My uncle sneaking into my mom's room, talking quietly. Their mouths moved and words came out but I couldn't hear them, although I read 'Olivia' on my uncle's lips.

My mom struggling against the man in the cowboy hat, screaming, tears running down her face. She fell to the ground and he pinned her shoulders. She kneed him in the crotch. Feet running, my mom's feet running into two muscled arms that held her as she wept. My brothers' father pulling the man in the cowboy hat off the ground as he held his crotch. A punch smashing into the cowboy hat man's face. He fell to the ground again, knocked out.

A ransom note. It flashed so quick all I read was: *If you want to see your daughter...* It was typed in large, bold, black letters. My aunt walking my uncle to my room. Her hands against his back as she pushed. My mother collecting her clothes, tears trailing her beautiful ebony cheeks. My aunt counting the days on a calendar. My aunt watching my mom walk through the woods to the houseboat. My aunt squeezing a dropper, a couple drips falling into a bowl.

I opened my eyes. My mind piecing the images together like a jigsaw. Nothing happened between my mom and uncle. They were planning something for my aunt, or discussing her anyways, but it was innocent. Olivia paid the man in the cowboy hat to kidnap my mom. He hadn't tried to rape her. Miss. Dresdan's son overhearing the exchange and unable to get there in time and warn my mother. She knew about their little affair and meeting place but they didn't count on my brothers' father hearing her screams. My aunt standing alongside her bedroom door, watching as I ran past her, not even noticing she was there.

My aunt was never a victim. She got pregnant on purpose, knowing Grandma wouldn't kick her out with a baby. All she wanted was Grandma's money. The baby didn't work, so maybe a kidnapping would. Her plans were all foiled when my mom died and Grandma learned about me. Her own daughter poisoned her with something until she'd taken it too far and nearly killed her.

That's why she'd healed at the hospital. Without the drugs pumping into her body daily she regained control of herself and healed up. Aunt Olivia couldn't kill her, because then she'd get nothing.

Her tricks weren't over. If she couldn't have the money, she could at least get me out of the way to win over her mom's good graces. She guided her drunken husband to bed, only it was my bed and he didn't know any better. She waited and pushed him over the railing. She was a selfish bitch.

Emotions whirled through me like a cyclone. "You're fucking bigots. Every last one of you. You're black! You hear that you twisted bastards? You're black!" I screamed into the silence of the house. My voice ricocheting off the walls. *Black... black... black...*

My torso fell backwards against the pillows and a laugh from deep down ascended from inside me, bursting forth from my mouth. They were as black as me. Poor, bigoted bastards never even knew it but I had the proof. I could sing it and tell it to the world, share my great grandmother's little diary and confession. I'm sure someone would love to have it. It wasn't a bad idea and I considered it as I contemplated tomorrow.

Malery was a drop from the same bucket as his mother. He'd be here tomorrow, and I had planned to exact my revenge, quell my hateful thirst. The house and money were mine and I was going to do what needed to be done to vanquish all the pain, betrayal, and agony this house contained. Everything had to be destroyed.

It's Craziness Cuz

"Fresh made sweet tea," I said as I put the glass in front of Malery.

He didn't even say thank you before he took the glass and swallowed its contents. "This house should be mine too."

And Grandma's money? I could argue that one and toss dirt in his face but I'd take care of all that later. "Maybe we can come to an arrangement. You could move in, live here with me."

He furrowed his eyebrows. "We should sell it and split the money."

I collected his empty glass. "We can talk about that later. Why don't you take a nap, you're looking a bit tired?"

He stood, unsteady on his feet as he wobbled and attempted to take a step forward, instead falling flat on his face. *Damn that must hurt, you could have at least made it up the stairs and into your room,* I thought with a loud sigh.

He felt like a sack of rocks as I dragged his knocked-out body to the bed. He wasn't light and surely gained a few bruises as I lugged him up the steps and pulled him onto the bed. My body was sore and I was out of breath by the time I got his wrists and ankles tied to the bed posts. Deciding I'd crushed too many sleeping pills, dropping them all in his sweet tea.

I pulled up a chair and waited. Approximately forty-five minutes later his eyes fluttered open and he attempted to move. Finding he couldn't, he screamed in panic.

"What the fuck?!"

"No need to use that kind of language, cuz," I answered, my feet propped on the edge of the bed.

"You little freak. What have you done?" He pulled his arms but the ropes didn't give.

"Nothing you didn't deserve. Nothing you didn't have coming."

"Untie me," he ordered, as if he had some power.

I stood and turned my back to him as I sauntered to the dresser. A little velvet bag I filled with a special treat for him was there waiting for me. Picking it up and the candle I brought them over to the nightstand.

"You crazy bitch!" he hollered, his body shifting in the bed as he attempted to free himself.

Placing the candle on the nightstand and keeping the velvet bag, I untied it. "I thought we'd have a special moment together." I opened the velvet bag. "Do you know what's in here? Take one guess."

"How the fuck do I know?! I knew not to trust you. I shouldn't be here. I don't need any money from Grandma. Liam and I run a successful business." I twisted his arms in the ropes, his head moving from one side to the other.

"Watch your language. I know your momma didn't raise you to swear, only to be a racist asshole." I lowered the bag, letting the sand, dirt mix drizzle over his eyes.

He squeezed his eyes and rolled his head to the side. "That shit hurts! What the hell are you doing?! Have you gone completely mad?"

"Dear, dear Malery, I have more for you." I grabbed the candle, ran my finger along it until I reached the flame. I leaned it over his chest. "They say hot wax is very sensuous. Do you ever do this with your husband? Wait... where is he?"

Malery blinked several times to try and get the sand out. "Untie me. This isn't you. The things I did, I was a kid. I didn't mean them."

I sighed as the wax dripped below his neck and over his chest as I moved the candle. He screamed, causing me great pleasure. "A little wax never hurt anyone." I wasn't sure he heard me over his screaming as the wax drizzled over his genitalia. "You weren't planning on kids, were you?"

When his screaming subsided, I spoke again, "This is great quality time isn't it?" I paused to give him a chance to respond but he only whimpered. "I have some really great news to share, cousin."

He took several short breaths, calming himself. "You tie me up, pour dirt in my eyes, pour wax over my nuts to tell me news." A trail of tears cut through the sand and dirt over his face.

"I found some old pictures in the attic and wanted to share them. Just one really. I think you'll like it."

I slid a picture of our distant relative from the nightstand. "This is our great, great, great, great grandfather." I held the picture above his head.

"I'm… I'm sorry. Really, we were kids," he muttered between breaths.

"Take a good look at his features. He's black." The satisfaction rolled from my tongue.

"My life wasn't so good either. Grandma loved you and at least you had a family that cared about you even if you don't remember them." As if his talk could somehow convince me I should untie him and let him go. My vision so many years ago with him tied to the bed posts, flames licking at his flesh, flashed through my head.

"Look carefully." I shoved the picture closer to his face and sat on the chair, propping my feet on the edge of the bed. "You see great, great, great, great, great granddaddy had an affair with a high-yellow slave girl. Great, great, great, great, great, oops! Did I add too many greats?" I paused for a second. He scowled at me. "Anyways, Grandma Ingrid couldn't bear any children and when that baby was born with snow white skin, she kept him for her own. Raised him up in this house. I bet he never even knew he was black."

"Where are you getting this crazy shit from?"

I chuckled and lifted Ingrid's journal from the nightstand then dropped my feet from the bed as I leaned forward. "Well, Ingrid left a journal detailing the entire story. You see, every plantation has a story buried deep inside it. You are as black as me!"

He struggled against the ropes. "Maybe she was crazy! Maybe you get it from her! We can talk. I don't hate you anymore. I was a stupid child. What else do you want from me?" Misery filled his words, but I didn't sense any remorse.

"I don't think so. I mean, is this really crazy? You kicked dirt in my eyes, kicked my shins, legs, called me dimwit among other names, and tried to harm me with a voodoo doll. I was a little girl. That is what I would call crazy."

"I'm sorry. I'm so sorry for all those things. I can't take them back." More tears streamed from his eyes. I'd waited many years to pay him back for all his crimes against me and now that I had the chance guilt was creeping into my head. I wouldn't let it. He deserved everything I planned for him

I collected the spit in my mouth and rolled it together, remembering Cole's words years ago in the voodoo shop. I spit it on his face. It mixed with the sand, dirt mixture making a rough mud and rolled down his cheek.

He closed his eyes and cringed.

"This house, this land, Grandma's money, all of it is mine to do with as I please and you are in my house."

"I wouldn't be if you untied me!" he rudely interrupted.

I lifted the gas can I filled earlier. "May the flames lick the skin from your bones before you breathe your last."

He screamed after me as I trailed the gas over him and down the steps and to the walkway. His screams permeated my ears all the way to the porch. I struck the match, its ember burning bright. I thought of all the deceit and betrayal my family put upon themselves. My grandmother marrying for convenience, both of them participating in extra marital affairs. One that produced a child.

My aunt Olivia and her jealousy and rage directed towards my mother and how that pushed her away from this place. Malery, born into a world of hate, grew into that hate, directed towards me. The living reminder to his mom of her guilt. It ate her up.

I was no better than any of them. Pain and death ran through our family's blood.

The flames licked the roof top and poured out the windows. Buried deep in the bayou, no one would ever know. The past blazed in my eyes as all the ferocious hidden secrets and betrayal burned to the ground. My family's demented history no longer existed except with me.

The blaze and smoke eddied into the sky, raining ashes as I walked away from the bayou for the very last time. It was always my real demon, not the monster who killed my family.

Set Free

A year later...

I dotted the final *i* and slid the papers across the table. Part and parcel, I'd sold White Oak to a developer with a vision of a resort, secluded, only accessible by helicopter or boat. Told them they could bulldoze right over the family cemetery -- after all, they were all dead. Only thing I had put into the contract was under no circumstances should they ever cut down, remove, transfer, or touch the cypress tree near the walking bridge where the plantation once stood. It was the only thing good in that ground.

It wasn't the money I cared about, I was free. The handcuffs of the past vanquished with a shiny future. Since the day I burned the house to the ground my *vision* cleared. No longer the grim reaper's handmaid I saw life, birth, happiness.

I didn't burn Malery down with the house. It crossed my mind as I untied the ropes around his wrists and ankles. "I hate you too, always will," I told him.

"But… it's like you said, we are both victims. Run, quickly. Get in your car and don't turn back." His eyes wide and feral, he didn't speak. Scooping up his clothes he bolted out of the house.

As fate or destiny would have it, or maybe it was that silly voodoo curse I put on him; I reckon I'll never know. He and his husband built a business buying, remodeling, and selling homes. He was on a trip visiting their latest acquisition when a storm rolled in. The weather so nasty he decided to stay put in the house for the night. In his sleep the house burned to the ground – an electrical fire. Nobody can escape the grim reaper.

I wondered if the reason he agreed to meet at White Oak was to try and make a deal with me on the house. He knew the potential of the big house. He could have remodeled it and made a pretty penny. I drugged him before we got that far. As it turned out, the land it sat on was a large fortune even with White Oak burned to the ground.

I went to his funeral if no other reason than to pay my respects. No sadness or remorse coursed through my veins as his body was dropped into the ground.

I returned to Florida and spent time with Miss. Dresdan, my only living relative. Even rented a house not far from her. It was there, enjoying a walk, the ocean breeze on my skin that I found a cute little boutique. Summer dresses hung on mannequins in the window.

Touristy knickknacks such as shell jewelry and sharks' teeth filled small racks above the clothes. A woman, her thick blond tresses hanging down her back as she preened, tugging at the sleeves of a shirt hung on the wall. She turned at the bell, her porcelain face and round blue eyes lit up – Greta. Fate brought us together.

After Ella Louise was damaged by the storm she returned home, finished her schooling at a local private school then tried her hand in college. Only it wasn't for her. After the first year she swindled enough money from her dad to start the boutique.

Greta solved the mystery of Ella Louise or rather she saw it. She was a twin, her sister Emmalane. There was always jealousy between them. Men adored Ella Louise, she had her choice of suitors but Emmalane wanted one man – Damien Hartley. Emmalane tricked Ella into joining her at the well. She pushed her in and ran back to the house telling her parents a lie. She claimed they were attacked and Ella Louise fell backwards into the well. She claimed her sister's identity and married Damien. In my opinion she got what she deserved. The story Marva told was slightly different than Greta's.

After she had the baby she ran back home. Distraught and grief stricken, she told her dying father what happened. In his rage his company purchased the Ella Louise Plantation and he sent her there as headmistress for penance. She spent the rest of her days righting her wrongs. In truth, maybe she felt remorse and wanted to be close to her son, Isaac.

I didn't know which version of the story was correct but sometimes ancestors had a way of divulging the truth. Ella Louise and Emmalane had an older brother, Emerson Pierce. Greta was a direct descendent of his.

I stared out of the window at the scenery below. It hardly looked the same. The helicopter blades whirred above our heads as it made a turn towards the landing pad. I wrapped my hand around the tiny, pudgy hand of my daughter, Cole's daughter. She had my tight, dark curls, and his dimples. Almost five now, she was my life.

I'd never thought Greta to have any motherly instincts -- I was wrong. Sometimes I wondered if she was a better mother than me. Daisy, our little beauty, had the life of a princess.

We stepped out of the helicopter and were immediately greeted by the staff who took our bags and directed us to our suite. It took the company a couple years to finish the resort. They left the natural beauty of the bayou untouched, only sculpted here and there.

Bungalows blended into the ambience and a large building filled the space where the plantation once stood. It held the front desk, gym, spa, gift shops, and a couple restaurants. After dinner we walked to the cypress tree and lay beneath it. The familiar Spanish moss hanging like nature's jewelry. I closed my eyes and took Greta and Daisy's hands in mine. I saw my mother's face. Not just her mouth or a blurry version of her, but crystal clear. She was beautiful with her chameleon skin, bouncy, tight curls, and a smile that went on for miles.

The journey of my life had taken me many places, through many clandestine discoveries, miseries, affairs, and ambiguities. A mixed child born into a family with a dark, surreptitious past. The lies and deceit fed on each other, growing each generation. Hate building like a bomb that finally exploded inside me where it discharged in an inferno of malice. I was all that remained of a family secret that was better staying a secret.

I opened my eyes and turned to Daisy. Her little eyelids shut. "What do you see?"

"My eyelids, Mommy."

That was my daughter, no sight, no touch, no vision, no gift. Simply Daisy. I closed my eyes again for one more glimpse of my mother's face.

The familiar soft mesh of leaves under someone's foot moved towards us triggering tension in my muscles. I reminded myself it couldn't be Malery. The footsteps stopped a foot or so from my head a female voice said, "Debbie, Greta?"

The sweet sound familiar from somewhere in my past. My mind raced, attempting to piece it together. I opened my eyes and pushed up on my elbows. The evening sun to her back, haloing her head, she looked like an angel. Dark, bobbed hair circled her face, bright eyes, and a familiar smile I'd missed glanced down at me. "Johnie?"

344

Chelsea Evan's Girls Volume 4

Prologue

I remembered nothing of my childhood. It was a void. The place all my bad and sad memories existed, separate from my conscious mind. My parents died when I was a child and I became a ward of the state while they searched for a living relative. When none were found, they sent me to live with the first family. I was completely mute and so they gave me back to the state. I guess it scared them. Charice – my social worker -- says my loss of speech was trauma-induced.

She placed me in a different home. One that had more experience with traumatized children. This family had an older child who was very good to me -- Phoebe. One day, while building a Lego village, I spoke. That day marks the start of my memories. I was six years old. It's like as long as I didn't talk, I wouldn't remember. I suppose there was nothing good to remember until Phoebe gave me something good to hold onto.

I stayed with the family who took great care of me. They loved me like their own child and my bond with Phoebe sisterly. It was my eighteenth birthday that marks the day everything started, throwing me into a mystery, and a past my mind refused to remember.

Chapter One

"**B**reakfast is the most important meal of the day," Judy called as I tossed my backpack over my shoulder. Her tone of voice reflected a mother hen watching over her chick.

"No time. I'm already late. I'm meeting Charice, turning eighteen stuff," I called as I pulled the front door open. A pitter patter of steps moved swiftly towards the front door and a hand touched my shoulder halting my rush.

Friendly brown eyes, thin wrinkles ebbing from the corners set inside her round face stared at me. "You're never too busy for breakfast." A small brown paper bag hung between her fingers. She wasn't about to let me go without making sure she did her maternal duty, even though it was my eighteenth birthday.

I grabbed it. "Thanks, Judy."

"You'll be home for dinner tonight?" she called after me as I opened the door on the white Kia and threw my backpack onto the passenger side, sliding myself into the driver's seat.

I unrolled the window. "Yes," I called and backed out of the driveway. Taking one last glance, Judy's full figure filling the doorway. I waved at her and sped off. She always made a big deal about birthdays and holidays and probably had a big dinner planned.

The strip of offices were a welcome sight to me as I whipped my Kia into a parking space beside the handicap since it was early enough no one was there to grab it. The door opened with ease and I rushed past the familiar doctors' offices, dentist office, and CPA to the back of the building where Charice's office was located.

It was a comfortable setting as I dropped into the red fabric chair I'd been sitting in for years now. My eyes, as always, went to the snowy painted mountain scene behind her desk. She'd been with me since my parents' death, took care of me, made sure I was in the right home. Today marked the end of that journey.

Gold-rimmed glasses framed her blue eyes, her hair pulled into a messy bun and cheeks as rosy and bright as they'd been every time I visited her for the past twelve years that I remembered.

A short-sleeved blue blouse hung over her shoulders and she smelled heavily of Entice – her favorite perfume. "Happy Birthday," she crooned, wrapping her arms around me in a hug.

This was it. The moment my life became mine. I was graduating high school in two days and next year onto college. She quickly went through the paperwork and asked me how I was doing, was I ready for graduation, college. She was like a second mom in many ways.

"You've come a long ways. You were one of my first cases. We've been together since the beginning. I'm not at liberty to say…" she started, riffling through my file. "Where is… oh my," she mumbled. She licked her finger, flipping pages, then glanced up at me. "It seems I've misplaced it. I'll get another one." She stood and exited the room, mumbling to herself.

I couldn't remember a time she was organized, always forgetting something. My file was left open on her desk. It was the size of a Stephen King novel. My eyes immediately went to the picture of a forlorn little girl. Her eyes hollow, no smile, wisps of dull hair framed her face. She looked like a ghost.

It took a moment for me to realize I was looking at me.

Beneath the picture was a police report. My eyes drawn to the word *fire*. She wasn't in the room so I could glance through and read the contents of the folder. Beneath the police report, a psychologist's analysis. I'd never been interested in my past but seeing myself triggered a curiosity I was suddenly keen on understanding. Considering my options, I could read through everything, but I'd never get through all the information before she got back. I could take it, but that might get her into trouble, and I'd feel as if I was betraying her trust.

I pulled out my phone and took pictures of the police report, the psychologist's report, and the photo of myself.

"I got another one," she said loudly.

I stuffed the phone into my pocket in time for the door to open. Her blue blouse fell over jeans and green painted toenails peeked out from her tan sandals. I avoided her face, riddled with guilt over taking pictures.

She dropped the paper in front of me. "This one is important. It ensures you get a check every month to help with living expenses."

I signed the paper, still not looking her in the eye.

"I have one more thing." From the corner of my eye she leaned to her left. Using both hands she pulled something wrapped in yellow paper with a white bow. "This is for you."

A present. Guilt ate me up, tied my stomach in knots, but I didn't say a word about what I'd done. "Thank you." I took the present and stood.

She leaned her head down, meeting my eyes. "Is something wrong? You know you can talk to me about anything." Concern filling every syllable.

I could but I couldn't. She was bound by some type of confidentiality. I adored and trusted her, but I couldn't tell her everything. She was a social worker and her job came first. I met her gaze. "I… uh… I'm going to miss you. That's all."

She brought a hand to her chin. "Why don't you open that?"

I met her gaze and pulled the gift closer, unwrapping the pretty yellow paper. Inside was a thirteen inch, two-in-one computer. My mouth dropped open. These weren't cheap. I couldn't believe she'd spent that kind of money on me.

Yes, she'd known me longer than I remembered knowing her. She made many home visits over the years, even staying for dinner. There wasn't a time in my life I didn't remember her not being part of it. "I can't take this."

A smile wrinkled the thin skin on her face. "Yes, you can." She came around the desk and folded her hands over mine.

Chapter Two

I completed both my finals and escaped outside. Above my head, leaves rustled in the spring breeze as I stared at the picture of the hollow girl. No wonder the first six years of my life were a void. My mind was consumed as I'd worked through my exams. It didn't matter if I passed or failed them because my grades in the classes were both good.

"Got some chronic," James said as he dropped onto the bench beside me, lacing an arm around the wooden back of the bench. Dishwater, unkempt, blond hair fell over his eyes. He'd lived behind me. For years we'd pushed up the loose board in the fence between our houses and hid in his father's shed getting high.

His mother disappeared when he was a baby. He lived alone with his disabled father. An accident at work injured his back. He was barely able to walk and on a combination of medications that included narcotics. Physically, he never harmed James, but mentally he belittled him. 'You'll never

amount to anything. You're worthless,'
I'd heard plenty.

I stood. "Not today."

He grabbed my hand. "What fun
is turning eighteen if you don't get high?"
he urged, always the huge pothead.

I blew the air out of my mouth
slowly in contemplation. "What's the first
memory you have of me?"

"That's a strange question. Come
on." He jumped off the bench and
walked towards the student parking lot.

The gravel crunched under his
tires as he pulled the three-toned, rust-
bottomed Gremlin off the road.

We ran to the lake. I picked up a
stone and bounced it across the water's
surface.

"Nice one," he said, pulling a
pipe from his pants. He laid it on a log
and dug into his pocket again. Finding a
bag of pot, he drew it out. He smoked
morning, noon, and night; always high. I
couldn't remember a time when he
wasn't. It defined our relationship.

He handed the full pipe to me.
"Six years ago. I heard you crying
through the fence."

Phoebe had left for college. I was
lost, couldn't imagine how I'd carry on
without her. She promised she'd be back
for summers and holidays and I could

call her anytime. James, that's how I carried on without her. We became fence friends.

That day he pushed the loose slice of fence and slipped through. My face stained in tears, he found a way to cheer me up, make me laugh. I think he needed me more than I needed him as an escape from his father. His father unable to chase him, James'd slip out the back door and hide in the shed. That's how he'd heard me crying. I was on the opposite side of the fence as the shed.

I inhaled deeply, drawing the pot into my lungs. After passing the pipe back and forth I laid back on the grass. A couple white cotton clouds drifted across the blue sky.

He lay on his back, his head touching mine. "I'm getting out of here too. Got a job, construction."

"That's good." I meant that. He needed to get away from his father. There was potential in him but if he stayed here, he was bound to land in jail. "I guess everybody moves on."

We lay for several minutes, silence between us. "James?"

"Yeah?"

"Do you ever think of trying to find out what happened to your mom?" I asked. His mom was a sore subject. Her case cold after all these years. No answers for him and no leads. She vanished, that was it. Really, I think it was the trauma that brought us together. The pictures on my phone could lead me to answers, but did I want to know? *Would they give me peace or nightmares?*

"No, she left us. I hate her."

The pain in his voice tiptoed over my soul. If I chose to read through the reports, I was on my own. I couldn't ask him for help.

Chapter Three

Like every other sleepy, southern town, it appeared the perfect place to raise a family. A quaint, quiet place where bad things didn't happen until a triple homicide erased that vision. Opening people's eyes to the fact crime happened everywhere. It had no preference.

A tall, thin man with a tight brown mustache stood behind a glass window. His uniform fit loose and his name tag read Deputy Greene. What a boring name. I sighed and counted my steps as I approached the glass window. I pressed the red buzzer on the wall.

"How can I help you?" Deputy Greene asked.

Anxiety bubbled in my guts. "I'd like… to speak with… Officer Sugda." The words caught in my throat. His was the name on the police report. My instincts fighting my efforts to relive the memories stuck in the void.

He ran his tongue over his bottom lip. "What's the name?"

"Chelsea Mora," I said as if my name was a bad word. In this town, I imagined it was.

His eyes narrowed as he picked up a phone. "A Chelsea Mora here to see you, Chief." He pointed towards the plastic chairs with metal legs along the wall.

Misgivings crossed my path as I considered running. The door wasn't far. It wasn't too late. I could get in my car and drive home to safety. I didn't need to do this. *No, I did.* My heart raced as a door opened along the wall with the glass window.

A dark-skinned man with a thick chest stood in the doorway. "Come with me."

The plain white walls and weak odor of pine cleaner did little to ease my tensions. I followed him around a corner then another. I wasn't sure I'd find my way out. After four or five turns he came to a stop, guiding me into an office.

It was far more inviting, with creamy walls and pictures of children, some young, others older. I imagined they were his children. A picture of a young couple on his desk. The man resembled him, and the woman must be his wife. I sat in a cloth chair more comfortable and encouraging than the plastic ones in the lobby.

He took a seat in a plush, ergonomic computer chair. "I haven't heard your name in a few years. I s'pose you're here searching for answers." His voice deep with an edge, a warning.

I shook my head, my words caught in my throat. Nervous, I clutched my car keys so hard the tip dug into my palm.

"It was a house fire, took your entire family. I'm sorry." His voice didn't sound remorseful, as if he'd rehearsed it, expecting one day I'd return.

"Do you remember them?" I asked meekly.

He raked a hand over his balding head. "I don't. They were private people. Never heard their names until that day." He leaned forward with a stern face, his arms resting on top of the desk between us. "It took people around here a long time to forget what happened. I suggest you go home and forget it too, Miss. Mora."

Forget, yes, I'd forgotten it all right. I shouldn't dig it back up but, driven by curiosity, I couldn't stop. If I left and dropped it my mind would nag at me. "I can't, sir."

He nodded then stood. "I guess you should come with me then."

I thought he'd show me a police report or evidence, something at the station. Instead I followed him through the maze of the police station, outside a door exiting the back of the building. He walked towards a cruiser and opened the passenger door. "Get in."

Streetlights on thick wires hung in the still, summer air. We swept past small houses with porches giving way to mailboxes and gravel driveways, houses so far from the road they could barely be seen. He finally slowed, pulling onto a dirt road, rutted and grown over with grass.

The car stopped and he cut off the engine. "This is it. Where it happened."

He pushed the car door open. I followed suit and toddled nervously around the car. The grass crunched beneath our feet as he led me towards a weed-covered patch. Twelve years later there wasn't much to see. The frame existed around the weeds and a sprinkling of wildflowers.

He stopped short of the home's frame covered in moss. "You were right here. It still haunts my dreams. A tiny thing you were."

My voice caught in my throat, the words came out breathy, "What happened?"

"The fire was intentional, but you wouldn't be here I s'pect if you didn't already know that. Gasoline was used as an accelerant. This was the case that made the Hurricane Killer famous, Miss. Mora." He folded his arms across his chest.

I knew about the accelerant but not the Hurricane Killer. "Was he ever caught?"

"He was caught alright, murdered, couple years ago." Satisfaction lingered in his voice.

I shifted on my feet. "What else can you tell me?"

"You weren't the only child made it out of that house alive. Now, I'm taking you back to your car and you're going to leave town without talking to other folks. You hear me?" he demanded in a strong, stern voice.

www.ingramcontent.com/pod-product-compliance
Lightning Source LLC
Chambersburg PA
CBHW031618180726
48284CB00005B/1602